Rival Street Gangs
Versus
The Accused

Rival Street Gangs Versus The Accused

A Novella

Paula McColm

RIVAL STREET GANGS VERSUS THE ACCUSED
A NOVELLA

iUniverse books may be ordered through booksellers or by contacting:

iUniverse
1663 Liberty Drive
Bloomington, IN 47403
www.iuniverse.com
844-349-9409

Because of the dynamic nature of the Internet, any web addresses or links contained in this book may have changed since publication and may no longer be valid. The views expressed in this work are solely those of the author and do not necessarily reflect the views of the publisher, and the publisher hereby disclaims any responsibility for them.

ISBN: 978-1-6632-3400-1 (sc)
ISBN: 978-1-6632-3401-8 (e)

Library of Congress Control Number: 2021925654

Print information available on the last page.

iUniverse rev. date: 08/11/2022

Contents

Foreword

Paula McColm's breakout novella, *Rival Street Gangs Versus The Accused*, is an extraordinary literary achievement that demonstrates her skillful and creative writing abilities. Her book provides a unique, insightful perspective on Latino gangs and their impact on their community and the legal judicial system. Ms. McColm's characters are engaging and genuinely reflective of the Latino gang lifestyle. It is a must-read for any avid reader.

GOEZ,
Fiction Writer of the published book,
The Wanderings Of An Ant

1

In the Beginning

In the probation office of the Los Angeles Superior Courthouse, Lola Wright, a gutsy black woman with her hair combed straight back, was seated at a broken-in wooden desk with a plaque of her name and title of probation officer. At the age of thirty-three, she had handled hundreds of criminal cases, from misdemeanors to felonies.

This morning, she was rustling through paycheck stubs and other papers handed to her by twenty-three-year-old Minor Jimenez, who's five-foot-ten, bald, and slightly heavyset. It was the beginning of the workweek, and he had arrived to her office wearing a dark blue uniform with his name sewn in blue on a small white oval patch at the top right of his shirt.

"After I copy these for verification, I'll go over the expiration of your probation with you. Excuse me," she said before leaving her cramped office.

Minor remained seated, and as he stared a hole into a stack of files on top of Ms. Wright's desk, he had a flashback to his arrest that had occurred four years ago…. It was a pitch-black night, and a cop in his thirties had his gun pointed at Minor, slumped over the steering wheel of a smashed-up 2001 blue Camaro, at the end of the Artesia Boulevard off-ramp of the 405 freeway.

Another cop in his forties shouted, "Police! Get out of the car." Minor landed face-down on the street after opening the car door. The cop cuffed him, pulled him up, frisked him, then threw him into the back of the light-barred patrol car while yelling, "You're under arrest! You piece of shit."

Minor began to come back to earth after Ms. Wright returned to her desk and spoke out with a high-pitched, scratchy voice "Awright, Minor, we can do this the easy way or the hard way." He looked at her with a furrowed brow as she continued, "If you don't fuck up, you won't ever have to see my face again; but if you do and show up here again, I will be your worst nightmare."

After she gave him back his pay stubs, rent receipts, signature form for a twelve-step program, and probation expiration form, he said respectfully, "You have my word, Ms. Wright. I'm sticking to my twelve-step program."

She raised her voice as she said, "Don't BS me. You better stick to what you're good at. By the size of your paychecks, that's fixing cars and not stealing 'em."

"Yes, ma'am! Thank you, Ms. Wright," he said. Then he quickly bowed out of her office.

While walking through the probation office, he got out his cell phone and selected Anna with her picture on his Favorites screen. Her recorded voice came on after a couple of rings. "You reached Anna. Leave a message."

He left a message after the beep. "Listen, Anna, hope we're still on for tonight." Then he added, "Pick you up 'round five. I love you."

After he hung up and walked into the hallway toward the lobby, a ding sounded on his cell phone. He opened her returned text message. "Sorry babe at work & can't talk now … can't wait for our big nite out! Xoxo, Anna."

Upon reading her message, he smiled, closed his eyes briefly, then mouthed to himself, "Thank you, God."

<hr>

Later that evening, El Tepeyac Cafe, the popular hole-in-the-wall Mexican cafe on Evergreen in Boyle Heights, was packed with regular customers celebrating El Día de los Muertos. Minor and his girlfriend, Anna, were laughing while they were finishing dinner at a small table. Anna Velasquez, a slender girl of nineteen with long black hair, exuded sensuality tonight dressed in traditional Mexican dress; whereas, Minor's hunk-like sexiness was understated by his snug-fitting Lakers T-shirt that accentuated the shape of his pecs.

Minor pushed his plate with half-eaten food forward, then patted his belly. Right away, she egged him on. "Oh, Minor, did you really think you could eat it all?"

"C'mon, Anna, have some faith in me." As he leaned closer to her and pointed upward, he said, "Mark my words, one day, I'll demolish the Manuel special burrito and have my photo hanging up on that wall."

"I'll believe it when I see it," she said with a coy smile.

Lupe, their waitress who had been working at the cafe for twenty years, was dressed in a black skirt and white blouse. As she swiftly arrived to clear their plates, she said, "All done? Well, almost, I see." She placed the receipt down on their table before picking up Minor's plate. "I'm dying to see your face on El Tepeyac's wall of fame someday and collect the hundred dollars for finishing off Manuel's biggest burrito."

"Thank you, Lupe, and it's gonna happen." He straightened up in his chair and said, "You can count on it."

"Oh, I believe you, Minor. I just hope it's not when I have my day off." After she cleared their plates, she told them, "Now, you two enjoy El Día de los Muertos together."

"Happy El Día de los Muertos, Lupe," they said as she was walking away.

Before Minor stood up to get in line to pay the bill, he told Anna, "I'll be right back, and oh, Anna, you look amazing tonight. I love you."

She replied to him, "Thank you. I love you too." After he walked away, she smiled as she sipped her drink.

⸻ ❖ ⸻

It had been an hour since the sun had set over Assumption Catholic Church, across the street from the café. Meanwhile, several customers remained lined up outside. Nearing the front entry, twenty-four-year-old Mario Gutierrez, dressed in a Broncos jersey, and his partner, twenty-two-year-old Angel Bernal, wearing a FUBU sports T-shirt, spoke in low tones. Their attire signified their affiliation with the Forever Boyle Avenue Gang.

"Damn, I could eat a fuckin' horse," Angel said. "Wish we got here sooner, but—"

"Yeah, right, but shit happens," Mario interrupted him. "Just watch your back next time and keep your head down, cuz Puppet rules Cincinnati Street. Them fuckin' bangers got it out for us homies."

After Mario and Angel entered the cramped cafe, they were given a table. Lupe placed menus down and said, "OK, guys, I'll give you some time to look over the menu. Then I'll be back to take your orders."

Angel licked his lips once he opened the menu, whereas Mario couldn't keep his eyes off Anna, seated just a few tables down from them. "Man, I know exactly what I want," Angel said. Then he asked Mario, "How 'bout you?"

"Yeah, me too, and she's right over there." He nodded his head toward Anna as he said, "Dawg, would I like to tap that pretty thing."

Angel looked at her, then told him, "Wow! Go for it."

Mario walked over to Anna, taking her off guard as he stood above her and made his move. "Hello, pretty lady. I'm Mario. Can I buy a drink for you on this special day?"

"Oh, no, thank you."

"Let me guess; how 'bout a nice margarita?" He bent over to whisper in her ear, "Cuz I know what a beautiful woman like you wants."

While remaining calm, she said, "Just go away. I'm not interested."

As Anna pulled away, Minor came and grabbed Mario away from her. "Listen up, do you wanna live? Then back off, like now, or—"

"Or what? Chump!" Mario yelled. "I don't see a ring on her finger."

Angel rushed over and shouted at Minor, "What da fuck, man?"

Minor swiftly shoved Mario into Angel. "You better hope I never see you around my girl again." He glared at them as he continued, "Like I said, back off *now*, before I destroy you both." He turned around, put down a tip, then took Anna by the arm as they left together.

The silence among the customers was extreme until Lupe arrived and confronted Mario and Angel. "Awright, you fellas gonna sit down nice-like and place your order or what?"

Angel slicked back his dark brown hair, then asked her, "You got any pozole?"

⁓⁓⁓⁓⁂⁓⁓⁓⁓

It was just another Saturday and the end of a busy workweek at Raymundo's Auto Body Collision Repair Shop in East LA, where Minor had been employed for nearly three years by its longtime owner, Raymundo Garcia, a tall and lanky sixty-five-year-old who claimed repeatedly to whoever would listen that he was a descendant of the Mayan race. As he methodically moved around his black Silverado, he observed Minor, who was wearing a face mask while he was buffing out the late-model truck with license plates of RAYS ABC.

"Good job, Minor. Hey, go ahead and take off early today." He jokingly questioned Minor, "Goin' to the jewelry mart? Ay, wonder why? Buyin' a ring, maybe?" Then he said,

"Hey, but, seriously, we're gettin' a shitload of cars, and I'm gonna need you here early Monday morning."

While Minor pulled down his face mask, he laughed it off. "No problem. You can count on me. Just going over to my sister's for my niece's birthday."

Raymundo nodded in approval, then walked to his office as he hummed an old standard song. Soon after, Minor cleaned up and clocked out. He headed toward the parking lot in a dark T-shirt and black jacket and got into his two-tone painted 1957 Chevy. After waving to his boss, he drove onto the driveway.

Several minutes later, he drove past Hollenbeck Park, then arrived at the house of his older sister, Christina. Once he parked his car in her driveway, Christina, five-foot-three with an athletic build and streaked short hair, rushed out the front door and sprinted off the porch to greet him with a tight embrace. "Oh, Minor, get your butt inside. Josie's been waiting way too long for you to get here, fool."

"Oh my God, I can't believe she's seven now. Better hurry on in, huh?" Minor followed her inside, then shut the metal screen door. Popular music could be heard coming from the house along with loud hoots and laughter.

<hr>

Mario and Angel were confiding in each other as they walked together in Hollenbeck Park. At that moment, someone bent down behind a parked car across the street was scoping them out. Slender-built Angel leaned closely toward his short and stocky partner as he said, "Yo, I don't know if I can hang much longer. I'm paranoid all the time since Puppet's coming down on us in our own hood."

Mario brushed off Angel's fears as he told him, "Dude, like I said, just watch your back. Won't be long before he's history. So, don't sweat it, awright."

Within an instance, a gunshot from across the street hit Angel on his right side. Then as Mario turned around and ducked down, another shot hit him in the back of his head. Both fell to the ground as the gunman ran away. Screams echoed in a distant part of the park where there was a small family gathering. "Call 911!" someone yelled.

"Get the kids out of here!" shouted another.

···※···

While the birthday party was still going on, Christina stood alone in front of the kitchen window that faced the street. As her eyes darted back and forth beyond the window, she said aloud to herself, "Minor, where the heck did you go? You told me you forgot something and that you'd be right back."

Her daughter, Josie, shouted from the living room, "Mommy, when can I open my presents?"

Over her shoulder, Christina answered her, "Pretty soon, sweetheart. Pretty soon."

···※···

Several days later at the LA Police Station, thirty-eight-year-old Detective George Rodriguez, in a dark suit and loosened tie, got up from his desk in the Office of Gangs Special Division and leaned forward to look at his reflection in the window that faced the street. He rubbed his cheek, which had an old scar below his left eye, then straightened his tie before leaving his office.

Moments later, he was in an interview room seated across the table from Angel, who had his right arm in a splint. Rodriguez was out to get to the bottom of the shooting; he began his questioning. "Listen, Angel, we already know that you and your partner, Mario, are members of the Forever Boyle Avenue Gang. Don't pretend that you don't know who wanted to shoot you down last Saturday."

"Hey, man, I wanna catch the dude just as much as you guys."

"Once again, who wants you dead?"

Angel came back with cockiness. "Huh, wait a minute, Detective. Ain't you even gonna ask me what the bastard looked like?"

"Right! Sure, Bernal, go for it. Describe him."

"Yeah, well, I got a damn good look before he took his first shot through my arm and chest. The fucker was a heavyset, bald Latino about my age, or a little older."

"What was he wearing?"

"Like I told you before, a black T-shirt with some white letters and a black jacket."

Detective Rodriguez struck the table with his fist as he demanded, "Names! Give me names of anyone who's threatened you and Mario lately. C'mon, think!"

"Dunno his name, but he was the same lil' bitch that threatened Mario and me on Día de los Muertos when we were at El Tepeyac's on Evergreen."

"Ever seen him before? What was he wearing?"

"Nah, never saw him before. He was wearing a dark Lakers T-shirt, and his girlfriend had on a sexy costume."

"Did you notice any tattoos?"

"Nah, didn't see any tats."

"Go on. How did he threaten you?"

Angel began to speak with a stutter. "Th-th-this girl was sitting alone, and so Mario goes over to pick up on her." He spoke faster as he continued. "Next thing ya know, this dude showed up, grabbed Mario, and c-c-crammed him into me. Then he yelled to Mario, 'You wanna live?' After that, he told us that he'd kill us if he ever saw us around his woman again."

While checking his watch, Rodriguez stood up, walked to the door, then glared over his shoulder at Angel. "Hang tight. Be right back with some mugshots."

2

Life Gets Complicated

Minor's boss, Raymundo, walked from the workshop toward his office while Detective Rodriguez stood in the open doorway. Raymundo greeted him. "Hi. What can I help you with today?"

"Are you Mr. Garcia, the owner?"

"Yes, sir."

They walked into his office together after Rodriguez pulled out his badge. "I'm Detective Rodriguez with the LAPD. I understand that Minor Jimenez is one of your employees."

"Yes, he's been working here over two years." He hesitated before asking, "Detective, what's this all about?"

Rodriguez gazed around the shop, then glared at Raymundo. "I need you to take me to him now. We have to question him downtown about a recent shooting and put him in a lineup."

"All right, but you should know something," Raymundo told him. "Minor's one of my best workers. My shop's been here over thirty years, and we work on up to ten cars at a time." He walked closer to the doorway and said, "C'mere, Detective." Then he pointed to Minor at his workstation. "He's right over there working on that El Camino."

After walking out of the office, Raymundo and Detective Rodriguez approached Minor as he closed a drawer in his toolbox. Loud equipment sounds drowned out their conversation. Rodriguez showed Minor his badge, then cuffed him before taking him to the parking lot. A forty-year-old LAPD officer by the driver's side of the patrol car opened the back door. The officer tilted his head down at Minor as Rodriguez said, "OK, Minor, have a seat. It's just a short ride to the station."

Minor got in the back seat, after which Rodriguez closed the door and sat in the front. Once the officer started the car, Minor looked at his boss standing in the parking lot. Then he bowed his head as they drove away.

⚜

In the early evening at the LA Police Station, Detective Rodriguez and Angel stood in the darkened surveillance room behind a plate-glass partition as, one by one, individuals began to file into the lineup room. "OK, Angel, each man is going to be called to step forward one at a time. Now, I want you to take your time while you look over each one, all right?"

"Yeah, sure. No problem."

Under bright lighting, five Latino men stood in the lineup; each one was just under six-feet-tall, somewhat heavyset, and bald. They straightened up when an officer in a separate room gave them rather loud verbal instructions over a mic: "OK, gentlemen, please continue to stand under your number on the wall behind you and look forward." After they made a few small adjustments, everyone remained quiet. "Now, please, turn to your right and continue to look ahead of you."

The officer continued at an even pace after the men turned. "And once again, turn to face forward. Thank you. Now turn to your left and look ahead of you. Now, turn back to face forward." After he turned off the audio feed to the lineup room, the only audio transmission went from his mic into the surveillance room.

While looking through the plate-glass partition, Rodriguez asked, "OK, Officer, can we proceed with the rest of the lineup at a little slower pace as each one steps forward?"

"No problem, Detective."

With the audio feed turned back on in the lineup room, the officer's voice came through loud and clear. "All right, the first man under number one, walk forward three steps, stop, and continue to look forward."

After the first man stepped forward, the officer continued, "Good. Now step back in line." When the first man stepped back in line, he said, "OK, next man in line, please walk forward three steps, stop, and continue to look forward."

Minor, next in line, walked ahead and stopped while looking forward. Angel blurted out, "Oh, shit, that's him!"

Rodriguez asked, "You sure?"

"I didn't wanna say anything at first, but, hey, man, there's no doubt. That's the fuckin' bastard."

"Sure, sure. Just hang tight and keep looking until we get to the end of the lineup." The lineup continued until the man on the end stepped back in line with the others.

As the men remained standing, the audio feed was turned off to the lineup room. Rodriguez proceeded to instruct the officer, "OK, have the second man step out again, and have him turn at a slow pace."

"Yes, the second man. No problem, Detective." The audio feed resumed in the lineup room as the officer said, "The man second in line, step forward again, and continue to look forward."

Raising his eyebrows, Minor stepped out. Then the officer instructed him to turn at a slow pace.

After Minor stood back in line, Angel clenched his fists while he glared forward at Minor. "He's gonna pay! Ya gonna lock up that fucka, right?" he sounded off to the rather cool detective at his side.

"Thank you, Officer, and that will be all for tonight," Rodriguez said while staring at Minor through the plate-glass window.

The officer signed off, "Yes, sir. Goodnight."

Rodriguez took a slow, deep breath before telling Angel, "It's been a long night. Go on home but stay close, and we'll keep you posted."

<hr />

In the LA Twin Towers Jail, Minor, wearing blue prisoner scrubs, was seated in a visiting booth across from Anna, wearing a floral-print dress. They were separated by heavy plate glass and using phone receivers on either side to speak to each other.

"Everything has been a surreal nightmare over this last week," he said.

"Believe me, Minor, we are all praying for you," she said, then added, "Please tell us if there's anything we can do."

"All I can tell you is that I pleaded not guilty at the arraignment and that my public defender told me the trial might start in the next few days. She warned me that the prosecutor's a real hard ass after she filed my alibi."

"I know you said you were at Christina's for your niece's birthday that Saturday. Don't worry, Minor. We'll all be by your side at the trial."

On the inmates' side of the visiting area, a thirty something-year-old sheriff's deputy walked by all the inmates and loudly announced, "Visiting is over. Time to go."

Minor placed his palm flat on the glass in front of him, and as Anna raised her palm up to his from her side of the glass, he told her, "Don't say goodbye. I love you."

Anna gazed into his eyes and said, "I love you." They stood up together. Then Minor was escorted away with the other inmates.

At dusk, Juan Diaz, aka Termite, sat on the bed in a run-down Westlake District hotel room reading the *LA Times*, pulled out a .38 Special firearm from his belt, and placed the gun next to him. As an established gang member in his mid-twenties, he wore a Chargers' jersey to signify his affiliation with the Cincinnati Street Kidz gang. While smoking a joint, he took a pen and circled the lower-third headline on the paper's first page: "Double Shooting of Two Gang Members in Hollenbeck Park."

He called his head gang leader on his cell phone. "Yo, Puppet, just saw the *Times*. Looks like da lil' bitch Bernal's still alive, and Gutierrez is in a coma. Ay, but not to sweat; they got some sucka takin' the heat." Before hanging up, he said, "Awright, out for now, bro." After taking a hit from his joint, he rubbed his bald head, then scratched the right side of his neck, which had a tattoo of the letters *C K*.

<hr />

In USC Medical Center's surgical ICU, Mario, whose scalp was wrapped with a gauze bandage, remained unconscious on a ventilator and connected to a cardiac monitor. Several bags of intravenous fluid hung above him, most of the IV tubes were delivering medication into his veins via infusion pumps.

At the foot of his bed stood Minor's public defender, Julie Bulla, who had graduated from Stanford Law School about a year before. Her mid-length light brown hair and green eyes blended in with her modest brown dress suit. Wearing a white lab coat with Neurology stitched on it in blue, Dr. Curtis Li, a well-known neurosurgeon, stood next to Julie as she inquired about Mario's condition. "Here's my card, Dr. Li, and thank you for meeting with me today. I'm the public defender representing the defendant in the case related to the shooting that took place on November seventh."

"No problem. You know, if he had been shot in the back of his head with a higher-caliber weapon, this patient wouldn't be alive."

"Yes, I understand. When do you think he will be able to wake up and talk?"

"As of now, we've been able to reduce the high level of intracranial pressure with surgery, medication, and a medically-induced coma."

"How long are you going to keep Mario in a coma?"

"Possibly three weeks or until he becomes stable. Excuse me, but I'm needed in surgery soon," he said before he walked into the hall.

Julie stepped closer to Mario's side. Looking down at him, she softly spoke. "Mario, I believe you can hear me. Please tell us who did this to you." She left his room after Dr. Li called her from the hall.

"Dr. Li, I appreciate all of your time. Would you please contact me and Detective Rodriguez when he's conscious?"

"Sure, I have your cards," he said as he rushed ahead toward the automatic exit doors.

A couple of days later, at Twin Towers Jail, Julie sat in a counsel room at a table with a thick file in front of her; on the floor, her worn-in leather briefcase leaned up against an empty chair.

A tall officer in his forties escorted Minor through the door and pulled out a chair for him on the other side of the table. The officer greeted her with respect. "Good morning, ma'am."

"Good morning, Officer." He nodded, then closed the door. He remained in the hallway and was visible from the room through the window partition.

"Hi, Minor," Julie said to her client. "Now, let's get down to business. We've got a lot to cover since the arraignment."

"Let's do it, Ms. Bulla. But first off, do you know the actual date of the trial?"

"OK, Minor, I know that things have been moving really fast since you were placed here after the lineup, but just recently, I was notified that the trial will begin after this weekend on Tuesday morning."

"My God, after this weekend—that soon? Excuse me, but how the hell—"

"Now, listen, that means we have to go over everything that happened in your life starting with the day of the shooting and anything you can remember before or after that day." Minor lowered his head and rubbed his moistened forehead as she continued. "Why? Because whatever occurred in and around that time will most likely provide us with some kind of significance in proving your innocence."

"OK, I got it. So, where do you want me to start?"

"Well, let's start with the restaurant, the place that you said you saw Angel and his partner, Mario, for the first time. You were with your girlfriend, right?"

His eyes started to mist up as he replied, "Anna! Yes, I was with Anna."

From the hallway just outside the counsel room, the officer looked through the surveillance window, then checked his watch while Minor continued speaking to Julie, who was busy taking notes and pulling out papers from her file.

RIVAL STREET GANGS VERSUS THE ACCUSED

That afternoon, a petite nurse in pastel scrubs stood behind the reception counter in an OB-GYN office as she handed a bottle of prenatal vitamins with a double-sided instruction form to Anna. "Sorry to keep you waiting. It's been so busy today. Oh, and congratulations, Anna. Dr. De Silva wrote down your estimated date of delivery on the instruction sheet and wants you back for your checkup in one month, OK?"

Nodding in agreement with a forced smile, Anna slowly backed away. While leaving, she looked with widened eyes at two women in their late pregnancy who were seated in the waiting room next to a table full of parenting magazines.

Within a matter of minutes, Anna rushed into Envy Hair Studio, where owner Christina was standing over a middle-aged customer seated in her salon chair. While blow-drying her customer's tinted hair, Christina shouted, "Hi, Anna! You OK? Did you want a trim today?"

"Christina, I have to talk to you."

"What? Huh, can't really hear you, sweetie. Just have a seat and—"

"No, Christina, *now*. I have to talk to you *now*!"

"What?"

Anna yelled, "God damn it! I'm pregnant!"

Under her breath, Christina whispered, "Oh, fuck!" as she turned off the blow-dryer, then quickly removed the hair-cutting drape from her customer's shoulders.

The well-meaning woman in the chair told Anna, "Congratulations, and I'm so happy for you."

Christina told the woman, "All done and no charge. You have a nice day, my friend."

In a flash, Christina pulled Anna toward the back of the salon, away from the other stylist and her customer. Anna began to cry while Christina held her hand and slowly stroked Anna's long hair with her other hand.

"Christina, I can't have this baby by myself. What am I going to do?"

"Now, now! You won't be alone. That's not gonna happen. Look at me! I know that you love Minor."

"Of course, I do."

"And I know Minor loves you. Do you know how much he loves you?"

"I know he loves me, but how can I tell him anything now? I can't believe what's happening. It's all too crazy."

"Are you going to tell him?"

Anna shook her head. "Hell no! I can't—not now. I just found out today. You're the only one that knows."

Christina chuckled as she said, "Yeah, me and that lady with the tinted hair. Don't worry. Hey, trust me, Anna! We're family now, and I'll be here for you and the baby every step of the way." She gently placed Anna's face in her hands and said, "We must have faith and believe that Minor will be cleared and set free."

"I believe you, Christina, but we can't tell Minor— not now."

While holding Anna's hands, she said, "So be it. We won't! I promise."

3

Faced with Adversity

On Sunday morning in an assembly room of the LA County Twin Towers Jail, a priest in his mid-forties with graying hair on his temples stood in front of ten inmates seated in three short rows of molded plastic chairs. With his head bowed, Minor held a thin paperback prayer book as the priest was delivering his sermon from the bible. "In the days when Christ was in the flesh, he offered prayers and supplications with loud cries and tears to the one who was able to save him from death, and was heard because of his reverence. Son though he was, he learned obedience from what he suffered; and when he was made perfect, he became the source of eternal salvation for all who obey him. This is the word of the Lord."

The inmates responded in delayed unison, "Thanks be to God." An inmate in his twenties with a silver front tooth turned his head and pursed his lips at Minor, seated in the row just behind him. Minor showed no expression as the mass continued.

Later in the evening after chow time, most of the inmates were in one of the living quarters of the jail called the *POD*. They sat at the several bolted-down circular stainless-steel tables with attached circular stools. The TV was blaring while Minor was talking to Christina on a dial-style phone with a hand receiver, which was arranged in a series of five other phones fixed onto a circular kiosk off to the back of the POD. "I just wanted to let you know that the trial will start on Tuesday morning at ten o'clock."

"Oh my God, so soon? I will be there. How you holding up there?"

"It's no picnic, but my public defender's pulling for me. Listen, I wanna know if you've seen Anna lately."

"Yes, she came over to my salon. And don't worry. She's doing OK."

"You sure? I miss her so much. I don't want to lose her. I know this can't be easy on her."

"I can tell you this: Anna loves you, Minor, and she's on your side. For God's sake, we're all on your side. I am, and Mama too. You got that?"

Before Minor could respond, a loud announcement was piped into the POD. "Lock it down. Time for head count."

"Hey, Christina, I gotta go. Give Josie a kiss for me. I love you."

"I will, and I love you too. Bye."

After he hung up, Minor made his way back to his cell through a cluster of noisy inmates.

⸺ ❧ ⸺

Just before dusk, Detective Rodriguez knocked on Christina's front door. Christina opened the door, and then he spoke through the metal screen door. "I'm looking for Mrs. Christina Flores."

"Yes, I'm Christina Flores."

"Hello, Mrs. Flores. I'm Detective George Rodriguez with the LAPD, and I'm in charge of the case involving your brother, Minor Jimenez. I hope I haven't disturbed you."

"No, of course not."

After she opened the screen door, he showed her his badge, then placed it back inside his suit coat. "I'm here to ask you a few questions that we hope you will be able to answer for us."

"Please come inside, Detective."

Once inside, Rodriguez stood close to an end table with a framed picture of Christina and her husband in military uniform. After she cleared the coffee table of crayons, she asked him, "May I offer you an iced tea or glass of water, Detective?"

"Oh, no, thank you."

"Then please, have a seat."

Just then, Christina's mother, Irene Jimenez, who was in her early fifties and of small build at just under five-feet-tall, entered the living room. "Christina, is everything OK?"

"Yes, Mama." Christina turned to face the detective, then reassured her mother, "Oh, this is Detective Rodriguez. He's working on Minor's case, and he's just going to ask me a few questions."

"Hello, ma'am."

"Hello, Detective."

Christina told her, "Everything's fine. Will you please watch Josie in her room so we can talk?" Her mother slowly nodded as Christina gently guided her by the arm away from the living room. Christina returned and sat on the couch next to Rodriguez, seated in an armchair. "OK, Detective. What would you like to know?"

"Mrs. Flores, were you with your brother, Minor, at anytime on Saturday, November seventh?"

"Yes, he was here at my house for my daughter's birthday party."

"Now, Mrs. Flores, I want you to please carefully think back starting with the time he first came over to your home that day." He pulled out a small tablet and pen while she took a deep breath, leaned back on the couch, and closed her eyes. As he waited for her to speak, he thought, *I hope this doesn't take all night.*

⚬⚬⚬

On a sunny, tepid morning, forty-one-year-old prosecutor, Christopher Fitzgerald, with dark blond hair, god-like chiseled facial features, and in a three-piece suit, strutted into his office in the District Attorney's Office. Once he was seated behind his oak desk with a backdrop of law books that lined a built-in bookcase, he spoke to his legal assistant. "Hey there, my trusty associate. Well, Brian, tell me, what do we have so far on Minor Jimenez?"

With a prepared brief open in his lap, Brian Eckerling, a tall and tanned thirty-four-year-old attorney with thick light brown hair, rambled off the details as if he were reading from a compiled grocery list. "Minor Jimenez, age twenty-three,

24

grew up in East LA, was picked up for auto theft with a felony evasion, and blew a .08 at the scene four years ago. After convicted, he did a year in LA County Jail. Recently, he was released from a three-year probation. Been working at Raymundo's Auto Body Collision Repair and living in an apartment in East LA for the past two or three years. Still working on any possible gang involvement."

"Not bad. We can have our detectives check into any possible gang affiliations. So, what we need is a slam dunk in this trial. How about going over his alibi again? Are there any holes in his statement that will allow me to nail him?"

"Yes. The statement of his sister taken by the LAPD detective shows a notable discrepancy from his alibi."

"Go on."

"She said he left her house for almost two hours, essentially around the time frame of the shooting."

Leaning forward with his forearms and elbows pressed onto the top of his desk, Fitzgerald boasted with an upturned grin, "Good job! Knew his alibi was bogus. Let's dig deeper into that."

<hr />

That evening, Angel walked out of Ramirez Liquor, on the corner of Boyle Avenue and Whittier Boulevard, and headed toward a metal-flake blue lowered two-door 1965 Impala parked on the street. He opened the door and handed a bag of booze to Trini, his older brother, in the back seat. He was just a couple of years older than Angel and had a tendency to laugh a lot; in fact, he would laugh at just about anything because he was usually buzzed. "Dude, hope you got the Cuervo."

Angel said with irritation, "Stop with the shit and move over." He got in the back after twenty-year-old Cool Homie, who was wearing a black knitted beanie and sitting in the front, lifted his passenger seat for him.

After Cool Homie closed the door, twenty-year-old Driver, who wore a long, heavy gold chain around his neck, pulled the car into the street while a continuous loop of the song "Low Rider" blasted on the CD player. He began to question Angel. "Was Ramirez's son behind the counter tonight?"

"Yeah, he was cool and didn't give me any mouth this time."

"Good. That's the way it should be. So, hey, how you been since what happened to you over there at Hollenbeck?"

"Shit, man, I don't *even* know where to start. All I know is the lil' bitch that did this to me is locked up where he belongs."

Cool Homie interrupted. "Dude, that's not what he asked. *How you doin'?* is what he asked."

"Go on, tell him." Trini laughed and said, "I know ya still hurt."

Angel jabbed his brother in the ribs and told him, "I got your Cuervo, didn't I? So, shut up."

Almost humble-like, Trini said, "Awright."

Driver added, "Heard you took one in the chest."

"That's right, but it went through my right arm first. At least I can breathe awright now that they took that enormous hose out of my chest."

Driver empathized with Angel. "That's fucked up."

Cool Homie asked, "No shit. So, who da hell's this lil' bitch that fucked you up?"

Trini threw in a comment. "Tell him, bro!"

"His name's Jimenez, some heavyset, bald mother-fucka, sitting in Twin Towers as we speak."

Cool Homie challenged Angel. "You sure he's the one?"

"No doubt." Then Angel reached to get the bottle of tequila from Trini. Once again, he was irritated by his brother. "Hey, genius, pass me the tequila and quit bogartin'."

While they were cruising down Whittier Boulevard, Cool Homie partially stuck his head out of his open window and shouted to a couple of women in short dresses who were passing by them on the sidewalk. "Hey, pretty mamas, wanna take a little trip with me?" After they kept walking, he said, "C'mon, hop in. Anytime. How 'bout now?"

A series of honks came from the cars behind them as Driver slowed down to a near stop in an attempt to connect with the hot chicks. Cool Homie shrugged it off as he stuck his head back in the car and told Driver, "Fuck it, dawg. Just keep goin'."

Across the street from Calvary Cemetery on Downey Road was the home of Mr. and Mrs. Jimenez. Minor's father, fifty-four-year-old Ernesto, had a copy of the *LA Times* in his lap while he was watching TV from a broken-in La-Z-Boy recliner. After a long day at work, he began to rant to his wife, "I can't believe he's my son, now that he's up for attempted murder. Why couldn't he go into the military like me and Christina's husband? But no, instead, he started stealing cars by the time he was seventeen."

She yelled back at him, "He's our son, Ernesto. Can't you believe that Minor had nothing to do with what he was accused of?"

"All I know is I can't hold my head up anywhere I go since his name's all over the papers. Where did I go wrong with that boy?"

"Maybe if you used the belt less and gave him more of your love, things would have turned out a lot different."

"What are you saying—I shouldn't have used discipline to make a man out of him in this town full of hoods? How different would he have turned out?"

"Right! You didn't have to beat the tar out of him for something like not rolling up a garden hose to your regulations when he was nine-years-old."

He waved his hand up toward her, then said, "Oh yeah, I remember you told me that you would kill me if I laid another hand on him back then. Please don't remind me."

"This time is no different. Don't deny your son now, because he really could use our support when he needs us the most."

"That's enough. I'm tired of hearing about it. Just get me another cold beer from the fridge."

"Go get it yourself. You're all out," Irene replied as she ripped off her apron. When he got up from the recliner and walked toward the door, she asked, "Where do you think you're going?"

"Take a guess! Going for a walk to the corner market for a six-pack."

⚜

At ten o'clock, the bells of St. Mary's Catholic Church were ringing ten times, once for each hour, while several churchgoers passed through the archway of the open double doors leading into one of East LA's oldest mission-style churches. A couple of cars stopped in front of the church and dropped off passengers before driving away. Inside the church, Mrs. Jimenez was kneeling in the first pew in front of the statue of the Virgin Mary. After she completed the sign of the cross, she sat next to her daughter, Christina. "Ave Maria" gradually faded on the organ as fifty-four-year-old Father Guillermo and an altar boy in his early teens proceeded forward to the altar.

While the Father bowed at the altar and completed the sign of the cross in front of the congregation, Christina leaned close to her mother and whispered, "Oh, Mama, God is on our side. He's always been there for us, even in our darkest hour. Remember?"

"I know, Christina. That's what I always taught you and Minor." She looked around, then whispered, "Shh! I must talk to Father Guillermo after mass."

"Yes, Mommy, we will."

After mass, Father Guillermo stood just outside the arched double-door opening and gave brief blessings to those passing out of the church. Mrs. Jimenez and Christina were nearly the last ones to leave, and he stayed longer to listen to their concerns. "Mrs. Jimenez, may God bless you and your family."

"Oh, Father, please pray for me and my family, especially for my son, Minor. He is in such a terrible place and in need of God's help."

"Yes, Father Guillermo, please pray for my baby brother," Christina said before speaking to her mother. "Mommy, you stay with Father, and I will go get the car." Christina gave her mother a light kiss, then rushed away around the side of the church.

Nearly all the church members had left before Father Guillermo told Mrs. Jimenez, "I know you are a woman of God and that your faith will see you through these troubled times."

"Oh, Father Guillermo, our family has had troubles for some time now. Minor hasn't been given the love and forgiveness from his own father in such a long time."

"Very soon, I will go see Minor, and we will pray together again. May God be with you."

"Thank you, Father, and bless you."

He looked toward the curb, then said, "I see Christina coming now. Peace be with you, Mrs. Jimenez." Christina pulled her car up in front of the church, and her mother walked toward her as he waved to them.

The day before the trial, Julie and Minor were seated across from each other at a table in one of the Twin Towers counsel rooms while a sheriff's deputy stood guard in the access area just beyond the glass partition wall. She told

Minor, "I thought it best that we meet to go over what will be happening at the trial tomorrow."

"I'm all ears, Ms. Bulla."

"The jury's been selected and will be seated first before the judge arrives. The prosecutor and his associate will be at the table next to us, while we'll remain at our table until the court adjourns."

"Will my family be able to be there?"

"Yes, of course. I spoke to your sister and mother and assured them that they can sit somewhere behind us. Minor, the main thing I want to stress to you is that I am on your side. There will be opening statements presented by the prosecutor and by me, in your defense. You must believe that I'm going to do everything in my power to defend you."

"You've done this before, right?"

She started to blush, then said, "Twice before, and I won those cases here in LA, where I was born and raised."

"I thought you were from up north in the Bay Area."

"I went to law school there, at Stanford, but my family and friends are all here, in a part of LA not too far from where you live."

"OK, I believe you've got what it takes. I just don't want to spend the rest of my life in prison."

"Like I said, Minor, I'm going to do everything in my power to make sure that doesn't happen."

The guard opened the door and addressed Julie as he lowered the sound coming from his handheld two-way radio. "Excuse me, ma'am, but I gotta get him back to main circulation now."

"Is there a problem, Officer?"

"Not really. Following a routine order just given out." He walked over to Minor and said, "Sorry. Let's go, Jimenez."

"See you tomorrow, Minor."

"OK. Thank you, Ms. Bulla." Before being escorted away, Minor nodded, then stared intensely at her while much deeper thoughts surfaced inside him: *Dear God, please give me the strength to get through this.*

4

The Trial Begins

On day one of Minor's trial for two counts of attempted murder, Chris Fitzgerald, dressed in a three-piece suit, sat in the criminal courtroom alongside his associate, Brian, at the table to the right side of the wood-paneled courtroom. Minor and Julie Bulla, in a brown dress suit, were seated at the table on the left. Through an open door in the front left of the court, the twelve jurors had entered to take their seats in the raised jury box. A stenographer in her twenties pulled at her short dress before settling in front of her machine. Anna, Christina, and Mrs. Jimenez were seated in the front row behind Minor, while Angel sat behind the prosecutor.

A bailiff in his fifties stood facing fifteen others seated in the courtroom. After forty-seven-year-old Judge Laura Elliott, with mid-length blond hair, entered and walked to the raised court bench desk, he addressed the court. "All rise. Presiding Honorary Judge Laura Elliott of Los Angeles Superior Court."

Everyone remained standing until the judge sat down and adjusted the mic on the desk stand in front of her. She looked over the court case legal document on her desk, then struck her gavel three times before announcing, "Criminal courtroom of Los Angeles Superior Court, come to order for the trial of the attempted murder of Angel Bernal and Mario Gutierrez versus the alleged-accused, Minor Jimenez, with the occurrence reported as having taken place on November seventh at approximately three-forty in the afternoon at Hollenbeck Park in Los Angeles, California." She paused as she looked up briefly toward Julie and Fitzgerald, who remained standing behind their tables, then said, "With both counselors present, Julie Bulla, public defender assigned to the defendant, and Christopher Fitzgerald, attorney for the prosecution. If there are no pending issues, we will proceed with opening statements from both counsels, starting with the prosecution."

"No pending issues, Your Honor," Julie replied.

Fitzgerald followed with his reply, "No pending issues, Your Honor."

"Very well, Mr. Fitzgerald. You may begin with your opening statement for the prosecution to the court and jury."

Julie sat down as Fitzgerald walked closer to the jury. He nodded and made direct eye contact as he spoke. "Thank you, Your Honor. Ladies and gentlemen of the jury, it is for the safety and well-being of all living in our great city of Los Angeles that I, as prosecutor, am here today for the senseless act of violence that occurred in and around a public park, where many families and their children gather together. None of us can rest easily until those that choose to attack anyone with firearms are rightfully placed behind bars, away from people that deserve to live in a safe community without the fear of leaving their homes on any given day. Through testimonies by the witnesses," he said as he looked directly at Angel in the first row, "and most importantly, by the victim, it will be greatly apparent that the defendant, Minor Jimenez, is guilty as charged for the attempted murder of Mario Gutierrez and Angel Bernal. Please listen carefully to all the evidence, as I'm sure you will make the right decision when it comes time to place your verdict. Thank you, members of the jury and the court. Thank you, Your Honor."

After leaving the ledge of the jury box, he walked slowly back behind his table before sitting down.

"Thank you, Mr. Fitzgerald. Ms. Bulla, would you please give your opening statement for the defense to the court and members of the jury?"

Julie patted Minor's thigh under the table before she stood up with her response. "Yes, and thank you, Your Honor." She walked near the jury box, then looked at each member as she spoke. "Ladies and gentlemen of the jury, I'm sure that the prosecution would like you to believe that my defendant is guilty of two counts of attempted murder even before all of the evidence has been fully presented and weighed here in this court of justice." She looked at Minor, whose gaze shifted from the jury to her; then she continued, "As Minor Jimenez's defending attorney, I am here to prove that, in fact, Mr. Jimenez is an innocent man and that he has been wrongly accused of the charges placed against him. Ladies and gentlemen of the jury, before you place your final verdict, I must implore that all of you keep an open mind as the evidence in its entirety unfolds throughout the duration of this trial. Thank you, members of the jury, members of the court, and thank you, Your Honor." Now positioned behind her table, she bowed her head toward the jury while she stood beside Minor with her hand over his right shoulder.

"Thank you, Ms. Bulla, for your opening statement for the defense, and once again, thank you, Mr. Fitzgerald, for your opening statement for the prosecution. Both of your statements have now been heard, accepted, and recorded here in the criminal courtroom of Los Angeles Superior Court." Each counsel remained standing and focused on the judge at this point while others in the court sat forward in their chairs. "We will reconvene with further court case proceedings this Friday at 10 a.m. Let it be noted that I have been presented with the list of witnesses. Court is adjourned." She struck the gavel twice before departing.

Several in the court were speaking among themselves as the bailiff escorted the jury members away. Chris Fitzgerald turned to his assistant, Brian, and said under his breath, "Another slam-dunk case under our belts, soon." Then he tilted his head toward Minor. "Hey, Brian, check it out, and take a good look over there at Jimenez. What a piece of work."

Minor turned to look at Anna, sitting behind him, then gestured to her with his hand over his heart as a deputy came to take him by his other arm. Through her tears, Anna gave him a gentle smile. Before he was escorted away, Julie told him, "We *will* fight this together." He bowed his head and remained silent while leaving the courtroom.

After entering the corridor from the courtroom, Julie walked briskly to catch up with Mrs. Jimenez, Christina, and Anna several feet away from her. "Hello, Christina and Mrs. Jimenez. Please, can we talk over here for a few minutes?" she asked while guiding them to a bench against a wall.

Christina replied, "Oh yes, of course, Ms. Bulla. This is Minor's girlfriend, Anna."

"Oh, it's so nice to finally meet you, Anna," she said as she extended her hand to Anna.

After Anna shook Julie's hand, she said, "Thank you, Ms. Bulla, and I want you to know it means so much to us that you are fighting for Minor."

When they sat down, Julie told them, "I'm glad to be able to confide in you, now. I know this isn't easy on all of you, but I want you to know that I'm here to answer any concerns you have, day or night."

Christina asked, "Ms Bulla, our main concern is, will you be able to prove that Minor is innocent? We just can't bear to see him locked up."

"Listen, I'm not going to sugarcoat the situation. Today was the first day of the trial, and you heard the opening statements from me and from the prosecutor." Without holding back, she continued, "Mr. Fitzgerald is what you call a *hard-ass*. He has a high rate of conviction wins under his belt, and this is just another trial that he wants to turn into an open-and-shut case."

Minor's mother shuttered as she began to speak. "Oh, please, Ms. Bulla! You are not going to let that happen, not to my son."

Christina held onto her mother's arm, then said, "Of course not, Mama. We need to keep listening to what Minor's lawyer has to say."

"Mrs. Jimenez, that's the last thing I want to happen to your son. I'm here to tell you that I'll be doing everything in my power to bring forth the evidence needed to clear Minor and to bring him back home to all of you, but I need your help."

Anna leaned forward and asked, "Please tell us what we can do to help."

"I know Christina and Mrs. Jimenez have my card, but I also want you to have my card, Anna. If any of you has anything—I don't care how small—pop up in your mind that might have some significant bearing to Minor's case, please call me. Day or night, OK?"

They all stood up as Julie handed her card to Anna. Then Christina asked, "So, what's next? The trial continues this Friday, right?"

"That's right; a list of witnesses was submitted to the judge, and the trial will continue this Friday morning at ten o'clock."

Christina said, "Thank you, Ms. Bulla, and we'll be here."

"That's good. Minor needs all your support. So, we will see you on Friday."

After Julie left, the three women stayed for a moment to collect their thoughts. Then Christina said, "We must stay strong for Minor from this day forward." Anna and Mrs. Jimenez nodded in agreement as they began to walk with her down the hall.

On day two of the trial, Judge Laura Elliott addressed the court. "Criminal courtroom of Los Angeles Superior Court, come to order for the continuation of the trial of the attempted murder of Angel Bernal and Mario Gutierrez versus the alleged-accused, Minor Jimenez. If there are no pending issues, we will proceed by calling the first witness to the stand to be sworn in." Both Fitzgerald and Julie offered no pending issues. "Very well, Mr. Fitzgerald. We will begin with your first witness for examination."

"Yes, Your Honor, I wish to call Detective George Rodriguez of the LAPD as my first witness."

"Bailiff, please call forth the first witness."

He called out, "Detective George Rodriguez, please step forward to the witness stand."

Detective Rodriguez, dressed in a brown suit and tie, swiftly stepped forward to the stand. While holding a bible in front of him, the bailiff began the swearing-in process. "Are you Detective George Rodriguez?"

"Yes, I am."

"Raise your right hand and place your other hand on the bible." The detective placed his left hand on the bible and raised his right hand. "Do you swear to tell the truth, the whole truth, and nothing but the truth in this court of law so help you God?"

"Yes, I do."

"You may be seated." The bailiff left his side, and Detective Rodriguez sat in the witness box next to an adjusted mic.

Fitzgerald approached him within a close distance. "Detective Rodriguez, can you please tell the court and the jury about your position in the LAPD and how long you have been employed there?"

"I am a detective with the LAPD, and I have been working as a special agent in the Gangs Division for the past ten years. I began working as a police officer five years before becoming a detective."

"Now, Detective, you have been assigned by the LAPD to investigate the case involving the shooting of Mario Gutierrez and Angel Bernal that took place at Hollenbeck Park on November seventh. Is that correct?"

"Yes, that is correct."

"As detective and special agent in the Gangs Division, did you determine the defendant, Minor Jimenez, as being the key suspect through your investigation? If so, why?"

"Yes, it was determined that Minor Jimenez became the prime suspect in the shooting through the questioning of the victim, Angel Bernal, as the sole witness and by Mr. Bernal's positive identification of Minor Jimenez in his mugshot and in a lineup. It's unclear at this time whether the case is considered gang related."

"I have no further questions, Your Honor. The prosecution rests."

"Thank you, Mr. Fitzgerald. Ms. Bulla, do you wish to cross-examine the witness for the defense?"

Julie rose from her seat as Fitzgerald returned to his table. "Yes, Your Honor, I would like to cross-examine the witness."

"Please proceed."

"Thank you, Your Honor." Walking toward the stand, Julie tilted her head to the jury, then to the witness while she spoke. "Detective Rodriguez, may I be so bold as to ask you how old you are?"

"I'm thirty-eight."

"And did you grow up here in Los Angeles?"

Fitzgerald stood up and said, "Objection, on the grounds of relevancy, Your Honor."

Judge Elliott challenged her, "Counsel, where are you going with this inquiry?"

"Your Honor, I'm simply attempting to establish a baseline as to the witness's expertise dealing with his specialty related to the numerous gangs of Los Angeles."

"Objection overruled. You may proceed."

"Detective, did you grow up in Los Angeles?"

"Yes, I grew up in East LA."

"I would imagine that you know of just about all the gangs that are in operation here in our great city—about how many gangs are there, and about how long have they been in existence, Detective?"

He responded without hesitation, "More or less 450 over the last fifty years."

"My, those are astounding numbers. I don't mean to dispute your statistical knowledge, Detective, but do you happen to know if the key witness and victim of the shooting, Angel Bernal, has any affiliation with a gang?"

Fitzgerald stood up again and said, "Objection. Defense Counsel is leading the witness, Your Honor."

Judge Elliott faced the witness and said, "You don't have to answer that, Detective Rodriguez." She addressed Julie once again. "Ms. Bulla, can you show probable cause for your question?"

"Yes, Your Honor, I can. Please, allow me to continue."

"Objection overruled, on the basis that the defense has logical probable cause. May I remind you, counsel, that you are treading in shallow waters right now?"

"Yes, I understand. Thank you, Your Honor." Then she continued, "Detective, please give us your expert opinion on whether or not the key eyewitness, Angel Bernal, is in a gang."

"I cannot fully answer that question since any affiliation with gang activity in regards to the victim has not been verified and remains under LAPD investigation."

"Thank you, Mr. Rodriguez, and no further questions. The defense rests."

"You may step down, Detective." After he stepped down, Judge Elliott picked up the gavel as she announced, "We will adjourn for a brief recess of one hour and reconvene court to resume with testimony from a witness of the defense." She struck the gavel three times before leaving.

5

The Testimonies

During the recess of day two of the trial, Minor turned around and looked at Christina and his mother sitting together in the criminal courtroom. With a puzzled expression on his face, he asked Christina, "Where's Anna?"

"Oh, she just went to the restroom."

"What? Is she all right?"

She said, "Yes, it's just a little hot in here. Don't worry, Minor. We'll all be back soon."

While looking toward the back of the courtroom, Julie noticed Dr. Li entering through the double doors. She spoke briefly to Minor before leaving. "Listen, Minor, I'll see you back here after the recess. You going to be all right?"

"Yeah, sure, no problem."

Julie met with Dr. Li, then walked into the hall with him. "Dr. Li, I'm so glad you're here. There's a brief recess before the trial starts back up again."

"I wasn't sure I could make it, but I am due back in surgery in about three hours."

"I'm sure we'll be able to free you up quite some time before then. See you back in one hour, OK?"

"Sounds good. I'll just go out to get some air until then." They parted ways for now as he went to the elevator and she headed to the nearby women's restroom.

Anna came out of the restroom as Julie walked toward her. "Hi, Anna. You feeling all right?"

"Oh, hi, Ms. Bulla. I'm OK. It's just a little warm in there, and I had to freshen up."

Down the hall near the courtroom doors, Fitzgerald was speaking loudly in front of Detective Rodriguez and a woman in her sixties with glasses and gray hair. "Excuse me, ma'am. I'm sorry, but you better stop speaking to the detective, right now."

"I'm afraid I don't know what you're talking about," she said after having spoken to Detective Rodriguez.

Julie stepped away from Anna to get closer to Fitzgerald as he spoke to the alarmed woman. "Listen, I know that you're one of the jurors for the trial that's going on in that courtroom."

"Is there a problem here?" Julie asked.

Fitzgerald replied, "Yes. This juror from the trial obviously has been talking to Detective Rodriguez, our witness."

"Oh boy! Listen, ma'am, let's get you back to the jurors' room and—" Julie said.

"Oh, I'm so sorry if I did anything wrong. I didn't—"

"Ah, don't worry, and we'll take care of matters after the court recess," Julie said, then winked at Rodriguez as she gently guided the shaken woman by her arm through the courtroom door.

Detective Rodriguez told Fitzgerald, "All she said was she respects detectives for all our service."

"How freaking nice. You know the rules, Rodriguez."

While walking toward the elevator, Rodriguez looked at his watch, then said, "Yeah, you don't need to remind me."

After the recess, the court reconvened, and both counsels stood at the bench speaking with the judge while the rest of the court and the jurors were in their seats. Soon after, the counsels walked back to sit behind their tables. Then Judge Elliott addressed the court. "It was just brought to my attention by both counsels that there was an incident that occurred during court recess which involved one of our jurors. Mr. Fitzgerald, would you please relay to the court what happened at that time?"

"Yes, Your Honor. Shortly after recess was called, I saw and overheard Juror Seven speaking to the witness, Detective Rodriguez, in the hall outside of the courtroom doors. What I overheard was brief in nature. I immediately interrupted the juror and instructed her to stop talking to Detective Rodriguez."

"Thank you, Mr. Fitzgerald. Ms. Bulla, I understand you were also present. Would you please tell us what occurred?"

"Yes, Your Honor. I overheard Mr. Fitzgerald, in a rather loud voice, telling Juror Seven to stop talking to Detective Rodriguez. She appeared a little startled. After Mr. Fitzgerald interrupted the juror that briefly spoke to the detective, she attempted to apologize. I did not hear or see the detective speak at any time."

"Thank you both for bringing this matter to the attention of the court. I must remind all members of the jury that it is never permissible to speak with any of the witnesses during the full duration of this trial because the selection of the jurors becomes greatly compromised. Reselection or mistrial can be the end result." Judge Elliott gazed directly at Juror Seven, who removed her glasses to wipe her eyes with a tissue.

Julie looked at Juror Seven, then said, "Your Honor, may I please be allowed to speak on this matter?"

"Yes. Continue, Ms. Bulla."

"I have spoken with my client, Mr. Jimenez, on what occurred in the hall that myself and Mr. Fitzgerald witnessed, and we feel that the juror's brief comment to Detective Rodriguez was innocent in nature. At this point, we believe resorting to reselection of the jury won't be necessary."

"Very well. If you and the defendant have discussed this situation in full, then I will accept your decision. And of course, I must allow Mr. Fitzgerald to voice any further input on this matter."

"Yes, Your Honor." Fitzgerald stood up and said, "If the defense willingly accepts this matter as closed with no further need for intervention, then I've no further input, other than I concur that the juror's brief remark to the detective may have been innocent in nature."

"After receiving dual acceptance on this issue reported by both counsels, I will deem this matter involving Juror Seven as resolved and closed." The judge shifted gears to address the court's agenda. "We will now proceed with this trial by calling the next witness, who is Dr. Curtis Li. Ms. Bulla, are you ready to call your witness to the stand to testify?"

"Yes, Your Honor. I wish to call Dr. Curtis Li to the stand."

After the bailiff summoned Dr. Li, he arrived to the stand and was sworn-in. When he sat in the witness stand, Julie slowly walked near him as she began her questioning. "Doctor, will you please state your full name, your title, and the medical facility in which you practice?"

"My name is Dr. Curtis Li. I'm a neurologist and surgeon at USC Medical Center and have been in practice there for ten years."

"And Mario Gutierrez, the victim of the shooting on November seventh, has been under your care in the ICU. Is that correct?"

"Yes, that is correct."

"Dr. Li, would you please state the condition of Mario Gutierrez since he was shot in the back of his head and while he's been under your care in the ICU at USC Medical Center?"

"He's unconscious and in critical condition that requires close surveillance. I performed a craniotomy shortly after he was admitted to remove the bullet from the parietal-occipital area of the brain and to evacuate the subdural hematoma."

While Angel sat in a second-row seat behind the prosecution's table, his eyes watered, and his lower lip quivered as Julie continued. "Are his vital signs stabilizing? Do you expect him to recover after he becomes conscious?"

"His pupils are equal and reactive to light now, but his vital signs remain touch and go. To reduce the energy requirements of the brain, which in turn reduce blood flow and intracranial pressure, recently he's receiving a continuous IV infusion of propofol, a form of anesthetic sedation. We may need to keep him in this medically-induced coma up to three weeks. Mario's consciousness could return with some deficits in his speech and vision if the tissue damage remains compromised."

"Thank you, Dr. Li. No further questions. The defense rests, Your Honor."

"Thank you, Ms. Bulla. Does the prosecution wish to cross-examine the witness?"

Fitzgerald stood up and replied, "Yes, Your Honor."

"You may proceed."

"Thank you, Your Honor." He walked up to the witness stand and faced the neurosurgeon. "Dr. Li, during your ten years of practice at USC Medical Center, have you dealt with many other cases such as that of Mr. Gutierrez?"

"Yes, I have."

"Can you give us an estimate of the number of cases— over a hundred or less than that?"

"I have treated well over a hundred patients involving gunshot wounds to the head."

"Dr. Li, can you give us another estimate of those you've treated with similar gunshot wounds such as that of your patient, Mario Gutierrez? How many patients have survived following surgery and treatment over the last several years?"

"Every patient is different in response to medical and surgical intervention, but I have documented most of my cases through our system known as Utilization Review. The patient survival rate has been revealed to be as high as 50 percent over the last ten years."

"And of the 50 percent of patients that survive, do they recover normal lives without, as you mentioned earlier, so-called physical deficits?"

"Again, every patient responds differently, but yes, many that survive may have residual deficits in vision, speech, or possibly paralysis of part of the body."

Fitzgerald looked directly at the jury and then at Minor as he continued. "And would it be safe to say that your patient, Mario Gutierrez, may have only a 50 percent chance of living and might possibly die?"

Julie stood up and said, "Objection, Your Honor. Counsel is leading the witness through speculation."

"Objection sustained. Strike counsel's last question to the witness."

"Thank you, Dr. Li. No further questions, Your Honor. The prosecution rests." Beads of sweat remained on Minor's face as Fitzgerald returned to his table.

After Dr. Li stepped away from the stand, Judge Elliott said, "We shall end this court session with the testimony of the witness of the prosecution. Mr. Fitzgerald, please call your next witness to the stand."

"Your Honor, I wish to call Angel Bernal to testify on the stand."

Angel entered the witness stand after being sworn-in. Fitzgerald looked all around the court before he began his questioning. "Mr. Bernal, would you please state if you were shot on November seventh while in Hollenbeck Park?"

"Yes, I was shot in Hollenbeck Park on November seventh."

"Could you identify the gunman if he were here in front of you?"

"Yes, I can."

"Is the gunman here in this courtroom?"

"Yes, he is."

"Will you please identify the gunman by pointing him out and describing what he is wearing?"

Angel turned his head toward Minor and pointed to him as he said, "He's right over there, wearing a white shirt, sitting next to his public defender." Minor glared back at him as Angel turned his head back.

"Let it be recorded by the court that the witness has identified the defendant, Minor Jimenez, who is seated next to Julie Bulla, his defense attorney." He walked toward his table as he stated, "I have no more questions, Your Honor. The prosecution rests."

"Yes, the identified is noted. Thank you, Mr. Fitzgerald." Then Judge Elliott asked Julie, "Ms. Bulla, do you wish to cross-examine the witness?"

"No, Your Honor, but I ask to reserve the right to call the witness back to the stand at a later date."

"Very well, Counselor." Then the judge told Angel, "Mr. Bernal, you may step down." After he left the stand, she said, "Court will reconvene next week on Tuesday morning at ten o'clock. I move that court be adjourned after all members of the jury are removed from the court."

Both Julie and Minor looked away as Angel, with his head held high, passed by them.

Seconds later, Minor fumed under his breath, "What the fuck! Am I doomed or what?"

Julie touched his hand as she pleaded, "Believe me, Minor, we will see this through together in the next phase."

"Yeah, whatever you say, Ms. Bulla. My life is in your hands. Why didn't you grill that guy on the stand?"

"The time is not right. Please try to understand that as I gather more evidence, I will call him back on the stand." After the judge struck the gavel three times, several people stood up and began to depart from the courtroom.

6

The Defendant

The following week, on day three of the trial, Julie Bulla began to build up her client, Minor, through the character witness testimony of his employer, who was on the stand. "Mr. Garcia, you mentioned that Minor Jimenez has been employed at your auto body repair facility for nearly three years. Would you please describe to us his character as your employee?"

"Of course. I first met Minor about three years ago while I was at a showing of classic cars. I was impressed with the '64 Impala that he restored and with his can-do attitude from the get-go. I told him if he needed a job to come to my shop. A week later, I hired him, and he's turned out to be the best employee I've had in years." Raymundo paused, then said, "Hey, I can see how they're trying to paint an ugly picture of him. Sure, he did something stupid over four years ago. Hell, I went through similar pitfalls before I learned from my mistakes. In fact, in his twelve-step program, Minor has the same sponsor I had years ago; he would never resort to the violence that he's been accused of today. He's disciplined and has an excellent work ethic. He'd have too much to lose; Minor has gained much respect from his family and friends."

Fitzgerald rolled his eyes, shook his head, and sighed while Julie continued, "Mr. Garcia, since Minor has been working at your auto body repair shop, have you ever seen him become violent while interacting with you, the other employees, or any of the customers?"

"No. I have never seen him angry or violent since I've known him, and Minor's always been very agreeable with the customers and the other guys on the job."

"Thank you, Mr. Garcia. No more questions, Your Honor. The defense rests."

"Thank you, Counselor. Mr. Fitzgerald, do you wish to cross-examine?"

He stood up and said, "Yes, Your Honor." Then he walked closer to the stand and posed his first question:"Mr. Garcia, how long has your auto body shop been in operation?"

"I'm proud to say that we've been fixing cars in my shop for thirty years."

"Well, now, have you ever hired an ex-con before to work on your cars?"

"As a matter of fact, I have on a few rare occasions."

"Were you aware that Mr. Jimenez had been convicted of stealing a car while intoxicated after a high-speed pursuit by police about four years ago?"

"I always do background checks on all new hires, and yes, I was aware."

"And you hired him regardless of his criminal record?"

"That's right. While being in business as long as I have, I've learned to trust my instincts before judging an individual. Minor and I came to an understanding that as long as he's working for me, he'd have to keep on attending his twelve-step program. That's it in a nutshell."

"No more questions, Your Honor."

"Thank you, Mr. Garcia. You may step down." After Raymundo thanked the judge and left the stand, Judge Elliott directed her attention to the defense. "Ms. Bulla, I have the defendant, Minor Jimenez, listed as the last witness for today's trial. I think it best that we take a ten-minute recess before we continue."

"Yes, Your Honor, agreed. I choose to remain in court to consult with Mr. Jimenez until court is resumed."

"Very well. The bailiff will also remain here until we reconvene. Court is adjourned for a ten-minute recess."

As the jury and all the members of the court departed, Julie placed a legal pad in front of Minor and wrote, "Stay Cool," then spoke in a lowered voice. "Minor, we need to go over our Q and A once more before you're called up to the stand."

"Ms. Bulla, no offense, but I'm ready to give them my side of the story."

"Just remember what I told you earlier: this prosecutor is known for his dog-eat-dog approach, so he'll try to break you. He's also out to be the next DA."

"I can see that he would love to convict me for murder. I think he's actually banking on Gutierrez not making it out alive."

"Please put that out of your head right now. Just stay focused. When Mario comes out of this and possibly becomes a viable witness, that is what we should be hoping for at this point. OK, Minor, here's your Saint Christopher medal that you asked me to bring to you today." He held onto the medal after she passed it to him under the table. Then he bowed his head in silence as Judge Elliott and the others began to enter the court.

The race was on between Julie Bulla, the lawyer for the defense, and Chris Fitzgerald, the prosecuting attorney, as Minor Jimenez took the witness stand.

Right away, Julie asked, "Mr. Jimenez, did you shoot Angel Bernal and Mario Gutierrez on November seventh between three-thirty and four o'clock in the afternoon?" As Julie posed the first question, Minor's mother, seated in the first row, held onto a rosary while tears ran down her cheeks.

"No, I did not."

"Are you in a gang or have you ever been in a gang?"

"No, I am not in a gang, and I never have been in a gang." Minor continued, "My dad made sure of that when I was growing up."

Minor's boss, Raymundo, with an open twelve-step book in his lap, placed his finger under the word *courage* in the Serenity Prayer: "God grant me the serenity to accept the things I cannot change, the courage to change the things I can, and the wisdom to know the difference."

Next up, Fitzgerald began his questioning. "Were you at the home of your sister, Christina Flores, located in Boyle Heights on November seventh from 2:30 in the afternoon until 6:30 in the evening? Answer yes or no."

"Yes."

"In Detective Rodriguez's report, your sister, Christina, had confirmed you were there, but that you had left at three o'clock. Then you returned at 4:30. Can you explain your whereabouts during that time?"

"I drove to Little Tokyo to pick out a present for my niece's birthday from a street vendor." As he answered, Minor stroked the Saint Christopher medal in his right palm.

"Sounds sweet. Can anyone verify that? Do you have a receipt with a stamped date and time from the vendor to prove it?"

"No. I didn't know the vendor, and I didn't get a receipt."

"Well, Mr. Jimenez, I'm trying to do the math as to why you were gone over that period of time just to purchase a gift." He paused, then continued, "Uh, let's see, I understand that the home of Christina Flores is located less than a mile from Hollenbeck Park and that Little Tokyo is about a fifteen-minute drive from her house. Is that right?"

"Yes, more or less."

"OK, for the benefit of the doubt, let's say it took you a little more time to park. Still, I find it hard to believe that it took you an hour and a half just to buy a gift; but I believe that would give you more than ample time to swing by the park to shoot down the two victims and make it back to your sister's house party."

Julie stood up and said, "I object, Your Honor. Counsel is using speculation as a means of placing the defendant at the scene of the crime."

Before the judge responded, Fitzgerald ended the cross-examination with his last question. "I withdraw the question, Your Honor. But isn't it true, Mr. Jimenez, that, in fact, you threatened both Mario Gutierrez and Angel Bernal with their lives openly in a local restaurant just less than a week before the shooting took place? Answer the question: yes or no?"

Minor had just gotten shoved into a corner by the prosecution, and he was forced into admitting to the confrontation between him and the victims that occurred at El Tepeyac Cafe a few days before the shooting.

———✦/✦/✦———

A couple of days later, in the Twin Towers Jail, Minor reached a new low; he had been agonizing over the recent turn of events in his trial. After he was called to the visiting area, he encountered Father Guillermo, who he hadn't seen for a number of years. Father Guillermo was seated in a booth as Minor arrived to meet with him on the other side of the heavy plate-glass partition. While picking up their phone receivers, they shared in a warm exchange of smiles.

"Hello, Minor. How are you?"

"Hello, Father, and thank you for coming. I'm doing OK, or as well as can be expected under these circumstances."

"Oh, Minor, how long have I known you now?"

"Oh, Father G, since my First Holy Communion."

"You always were a resilient lad. Your family is very concerned over what you are going through, and I had to come see you and to listen to your hopes and fears."

"Father, I appreciate all your thoughts and prayers and for being at my trial the other day."

"I know that this is the biggest life hurdle that you are going through right now. Please know that I'm here if you need me to pray with you."

"Yes, Father, could you please quote something from the bible that will provide me with some strength?"

"Let us bow our heads and close our eyes to pray together. Taken from the Holy Scripture of Second Corinthians in the New Testament, 'Our Lord's message to the faithful: In the time of meeting with our greatest adversities, He will not give us more than we can bear.' We pray this together for your son, Minor, follower of Jesus Christ. Please, provide him with your strength during this time while his faith is being challenged by wrongdoers. O dear Lord, we believe that you will not allow him to experience trials and tribulations beyond what he can bear. We pray this, in the name of the Father, the Son, and the Holy Spirit. Amen."

After opening their eyes, they maintained a brief moment of silence together. Then Minor said, "Thank you, Father."

"God bless you, Minor, and know that our thoughts and prayers will be with you. Listen, on a lighter note before I leave, is Raymundo's shop in the same spot it was over thirty years ago?"

"Yes, it sure is."

"Think I need to pay him a visit. A couple of young boys crashed their skateboards into the back fender of our car parked near the church rectory."

"Oh, go on over, Father. He'll take good care of you there."

"I'm sure he will."

The following day, Father G parked his 2002 black Honda Accord in the parking lot of the auto body repair shop while Raymundo was standing just outside the garage opening. Father G waved to Raymundo as he got out of his car.

"Hello, Mr. Garcia. I'm looking for an estimate on a fender bender."

"You came to the right place, Father. Let's take a look."

They walked to the driver's side of the rear fender to check it out. "Let me guess—someone in a bad mood took a hammer to it?"

"Not quite. A couple of hyperactive skateboarders got off track."

Raymundo chuckled as he said, "Makes sense. Well, it shouldn't cost much. When do you want it back?"

"Uh, I could spare it for a week."

"That's no problem, and we can have it back to you before then if you want to bring it back tomorrow. So, Father, are you sure I can't help you with something else?"

"From what I've seen, you have been of tremendous help to the Jimenez family, and I hope we can discuss more helpful things that we could accomplish together. But, first things first, let's see you perform a little tender, loving care on good old Bessie here."

With a sly grin, Raymundo said, "I catch your drift, and no problem, Father. Just stop by tomorrow."

Father Guillermo slipped back into his car and shut the door. Before leaving, he spoke through his open window. "Yes. I knew we could count on you. See you tomorrow, Raymundo."

It was early evening and another grueling day for Julie. She was leaving the LA Superior Courthouse with her bulky briefcase. In the parking lot, she caught up with thirty-five-year-old Andrea Lifton, a five-foot-five redhead who was notorious for being outspoken and one of the best-dressed attorneys in town. Today, she was wearing an off-white Chanel dress suit.

Andrea placed a box of files in the trunk of her late-model black Lexus. Then she commented to Julie, "Listen, I think you're really taking this case way too seriously."

"I can't help it. I thought I'd die the other day in court when he told me, 'Whatever you say; my life is in your hands.'"

"Go on—really? Well, I don't think this Jimenez guy's too far off. Why do you think they call it the *practice* of law? We keep at it until, hopefully, we get it right." After Andrea closed the trunk, she asked, "You know what you need?"

"No. What, Counselor?"

"A good lay! And don't gimme that innocent look."

"Oh, come on!"

"I mean it. I know you haven't been gettin' out much, and it's high time you have some fun for a change."

Julie grinned and said, "Yeah, right! I gotta get going."

After opening her car door, Andrea gave the peace sign. Then Julie walked down the way toward her silver VW Bug.

7

A Take on Family

It was early evening as Christina rushed into her living room after hearing the phone ring. "Oh, hi, Father Guillermo," she said upon answering his call.

"Christina, I hate to bother you with this right now, but I need to ask a favor of you."

"Sure. What is it?"

"Well, my car just got repaired, and I can't seem to find anyone available to give me a lift to pick it up tomorrow at the shop. I wasn't sure if you or your mother would be willing to drop me off, if you're not too busy."

"Oh, Father, I would if I could, but over the holidays, we've been nonstop at my salon."

"I hear you. Same here at the church. Is your mother or father doing anything tomorrow?"

"Oh, my mother doesn't really drive anymore. But wait, I'm sure my dad can help you out. He's usually free in the morning. I'll give you a call back after I check with him, OK?"

"That would be great. Thank you, and bye for now."

"Bye, Father." She hung up, started dialing her parents' home, and waited for an answer as the phone rang.

—⁂—

Early the next morning, Minor's dad, Ernesto, was driving Father Guillermo in his 2010 white Ford Bronco en route to Raymundo's shop.

"Mr. Jimenez, I can't tell you how much I appreciate you giving me a lift to the shop."

"Oh, don't worry about it, Father. So, how much farther to make a right did you say?"

"Oh, yes, let me see. We're getting close. OK, now, don't turn at this light. But at the next light, make a right; then you can't miss it. His shop will be just a couple of driveways down."

"Hope they took good care of your car for you."

"Oh, sure, he's one of the best in town when it comes to body repair."

Ernesto pointed ahead and asked, "Is this it?"

They were right in front of the driveway to Raymundo's shop as Father Guillermo said, "Yes, this is it. Just pull in. Oh, and would you mind accompanying me into the office, if you have a few minutes?"

Ernesto nodded as he parked in the lot. Then they got out and walked to the office.

Raymundo was standing at his desk talking on the phone with a customer. He waved as Father Guillermo arrived with Ernesto. While they were waiting for him to finish his call, Ernesto looked around, then stared up at a framed photo of a young man in an Army uniform with a small plaque on the wall. "Yes, sir, and I look forward to seeing you. Oh, by the way, we're open till six o'clock. Bye now." After he hung up, Raymundo was all smiles. "Hello, Father. Happy to see you again, and how are you?"

"I'm just fine, Raymundo, and guess you know why I'm here, right?"

"Of course. Your vehicle is ready and waiting for pickup. Want to check her out?"

"Sure, sure, but first, I want to introduce you to an old friend. Raymundo, this is Ernesto Jimenez."

"Nice to meet you, Ernesto."

He looked again at the framed photo overhead and pointed to it. Then he asked Raymundo, "Is that a portrait of your son?"

"Yes, it is."

Ernesto took off his Army baseball cap, then said, "I knew your son, Private Ruben Garcia, while he served in our squad in Iraq. He was a fine young man and a brave soldier. I'm so sorry for your loss."

"Thank you for your condolences. He used to write to me about how he respected you as his superior. I gotta say that I think of Ruben as though he's still here."

Raymundo's thirty-year-old employee, Beto, came in and asked, "Excuse me, Raymundo. Did you want me to drive Father's car out now?"

"Yes, Beto. Just park it out front, please." Then he told Father G, "I'll be glad to walk you out to inspect your Honda."

"Sure. I'll meet you over there."

After Beto and Father left, Raymundo and Ernesto had a brief interaction. "I had no idea that Ruben was your son until now."

"And I had no idea that Minor was your son until a year or so after I hired him. We must remain strong for both of our sons. Don't you agree?"

Ernesto put his baseball cap back on, shook hands with Raymundo, then somberly nodded in agreement.

———⌇∿⌇———

In the afternoon, Anna was at her doctor's office, lying on an exam table in a patient gown, as forty-five-year-old Dr. De Silva, with jet black hair, was at her side. "Anna, I'm glad you came in after you reported that you've had some spotting of blood. For how many days?"

"About two days."

"And you said it was very light in color, not bright red?"

"Yes, Doctor, it's pinkish-red and just a few spots here and there."

"I must ask you if you've been under any stress lately."

"Doctor, you know that I'm not married," she said timidly.

"Are you in a relationship with the father? How do you both feel about the baby?"

"He doesn't know that I'm pregnant. I couldn't tell him."

"Anna, I need to ask you, *Why?*"

She began to cry and was unable to speak. He came closer to hold her hand as she started to open up. "I love him, and I know that he loves me; but everything has changed since he was arrested."

"Oh, Anna, I'm sorry. What was he arrested for?"

"I still can't believe it, but he was accused of shooting two men. And I know he didn't do it because he would never do such a thing."

"Anna, do you want to have this baby?"

She started bawling as she said, "Yes, yes, I want our baby."

Dr. De Silva held her by the shoulders, and then went to the door and opened it. He called out into the hall to his nurse, who was in her thirties and had light brown hair. "Judy, please come in here now." His nurse arrived, walked over to Anna, helped her turn onto her side, and lightly rubbed her back.

"Please know that we need to watch your condition closely right now." When Anna's crying subsided, he continued, "Sometimes, light bleeding can happen early in pregnancy, but just to be on the safe side, I want you to go on bed rest." Then he asked, "Is anyone here with you today?"

"Yes, Minor's sister, Christina."

"She's in the waiting room, Doctor," his nurse said.

"Please bring her in Judy." After Judy left, he started writing down his orders.

"Hello, Doctor. Is Anna going to be all right?" Christina asked after Judy escorted her into the exam room.

"Yes and no. I want Anna to stay on bed rest for a week while we monitor her light spotting." Then he asked, "Can you or anyone in the family help in her care right now?"

"Yes, I can stay with her and watch over her."

"I'm going to order a visiting nurse to come out for home visits to check on her condition." He turned to his nurse, handed her his orders, and said, "Judy, please go over all the instructions with both Anna and Christina, and get their address info before they drive home."

She nodded. "Yes, Dr. De Silva, I will."

"Family support is most important. Anna, I believe you will find a way to work through this, but you must stay in bed for now." After both women thanked him, he patted Anna's hand and nodded at Christina before leaving the room.

<hr>

After a long, trying morning, Julie was on her way out of the Superior Court building. As her cell phone began to ring, she pulled it out of the pocket of her blazer and answered it. "Hello?"

"Hello, Ms. Bulla. This is Anna Velasquez, Minor's girlfriend." She was propped up in bed while speaking on the phone.

"Oh, hello, Anna. How are you?" Somewhat surprised, Julie went back into the court building and stood away from the busy foot traffic.

Anna's voice became shaky as she continued. "Ms. Bulla, I've been very worried about Minor. I know that you are doing everything you can to defend him, but I had to call you."

"OK, take a few deep breaths and try to tell me what's on your mind."

"I just can't hide it from him anymore, and when you gave me your card, you told me to call you if anything popped up. And, uh …"

"Anna, let's take this one step at a time. What is it that you're worried about? And what is it that you've been hiding from Minor?"

"Remember the last time you saw me when I was coming out of the restroom during Minor's trial?"

"Yes, and you looked very pale that day. Yes, I remember."

"Well, I was having morning sickness. I haven't been able to tell Minor that I'm pregnant because of his trial. I just didn't know how."

"Oh, Anna, I understand, but please tell me that you're all right. Have you seen a doctor?"

"That's why I'm calling you now. I left the doctor's office, and he ordered me to stay on bed rest right now because I had a little blood spotting lately. So, I'm staying at Christina's now."

"OK. Now listen. Minor is very strong, and the truth shouldn't be hidden from him anymore, because he loves you very much. I can meet with him soon to break the news to him, but you must rest and not get stressed out."

"I know you're right. I'm so sorry about having to call you like this."

"I'm glad you turned to me. Thank goodness that Christina is there with you. We'll stay in close touch from here on out, and I'll call both you and Christina soon."

"Thank you, Ms. Bulla."

"You're welcome, Anna, and bye for now." After hanging up, Julie took a few steps around the lobby, then called Andrea.

"Hello?"

"Hi, Andrea."

"Well, well, Julie! What's up?"

"Hey, listen, I'm near your office right now and wondering if I can take you out for lunch."

"Well, just so happens I'll be freed up within an hour. How about sushi?"

"I know the place, just across the street from your office, right?"

"You read my mind. Anything in particular that you want to discuss?"

"To be honest, I could use some sound advice about this case that's turning into a handful. Uh, by the way, do you still assist with legal cases on a pro-bono basis?"

"All depends on the case. Perhaps we can talk it through over a little sake."

"Love your idea. Thanks, Andrea, and see you soon." After she hung up, she said, "Yes!" aloud. While she checked her Visa card in her wallet, she thought, *How the hell am I going to prove Minor's innocence? I can't do this on my own.*

8

Hanging in the Balance

At USC Medical Center, a relief staff nurse in her late twenties walked into Mario's room. Seeing that his cardiac monitor wavelength displayed ventricular tachycardia at a rate of 250, she pressed the Code Blue button above the head of his bed. She checked his pulse, then yelled into the hall, "Code Blue, room six!"

"Code Blue, Surgical ICU" was announced several times in the halls via the PA system as the thirty-something charge nurse, wearing a white lab coat, rolled a crash cart into the room with other staff members following behind her.

Within a couple of minutes, an intern in his twenties and a thirty-year-old resident also ran into the room. "Nurse, give me a general assessment," ordered the resident.

The charge nurse provided the patient's overall status. "Mario Gutierrez, twenty-four, went into V-tach with no pulse. Patient's been on the vent, then placed on continuous IV propofol nearly three weeks ago. Evacuation of subdural hematoma by neurosurgeon Dr. Li was on November seventh post gunshot wound to the head."

The resident called out, "Call Dr. Li stat. Continue chest compressions and O_2 ventilation via Ambu bag." Then he asked, "What's his BP and intracranial pressure?"

The relief nurse replied, "Forty systolic, and ICP within normal past twenty-four hours."

"Turn off IV propofol. Stop compressions. Check for pulse."

"No pulse," said the relief nurse.

"Continue CPR. Charge defibrillator to 300 watts per second. Any meds given?"

The charge nurse replied, "IV bolus of lidocaine with lidocaine IV drip started, and a dopamine IV drip just started."

The respiratory therapist drew blood from the arterial line, and the intern applied gel pads to Mario's chest as the resident kept calling out orders. "Give a milligram of epi now, then two amps of IV bicarb. Get an arterial blood gas stat and a full chemistry panel with a CBC." The defibrillator became fully charged as the resident continued. "Stop CPR; remove the O_2. All clear."

Everyone stepped back from the bed. The relief nurse delivered the charge to his chest. Then the intern placed his fingers over Mario's carotid artery to check for a pulse. As the intern shook his head *no*, the cardiac wavelength displayed ventricular fib.

The resident continued his orders in rapid succession. "Give another milligram of epinephrine and continue CPR. Give another bolus of lidocaine and up the IV drip to 60 cc an hour. Titrate IV dopamine to bring up his BP. Up the charge to 360 watts per second. All clear and defib at 360 *now*."

Mario Gutierrez had now approached a near-death experience. He began looking down at his body from a bird's-eye viewpoint as the healthcare team continued resuscitation efforts. Beeping alarms and the voices of the doctors and nurses became echo-like, then discernible as Mario floated through the ceiling away from the ICU room. He started walking through a darkened tunnel-like space that became more lit as he went forward.

Mario turned his head and looked at Angel, who was now walking alongside him, and asked, "Angel, what are we doing here?"

"I dunno, Mario. I think I really fucked up."

"What do you mean?" At that, Angel was no longer by his side.

Mario walked closer to the light bursting in front of him as his father, who had died three years ago at the age of forty-four, appeared to him. "Pop! Is that you?"

"Mario, I miss you. Go back and do what is right, my son."

"Don't go, Pop."

As Mario was being pulled away, he quickly came to a halt in front of a young Latino soldier resembling Private Ruben Garcia. "Who are you?"

He replied, "It doesn't matter, Mario. I fought for freedom, and now we need you to fight for justice. Go back, and do the right thing for our brother."

All of Mario's visual images started to fade away; then the sound of beeping alarms and the voices of the hospital staff returned in full force. "Give him calcium chloride IV push, run in IV fluids, and stop CPR to check for pulse—"

The intern shouted, "He's in bradycardia!" Then he placed his fingers over Mario's neck and said, "I feel a pulse."

<hr />

That same day, several empty beer bottles were scattered on the floor in Trini's apartment as Trini, in a wife-beater underwear shirt, stumbled in from the hall while yelling out to Cool Homie, who was asleep on a worn-out crushed-velvet sofa. "Hey, wake the fuck up. Help!"

Cool Homie woke up and said, "What the hell?"

"Call 911. It's Angel. I don't think he's breathin'."

Cool Homie jumped up and ran into the bedroom, where he got down on the floor next to Angel, then vigorously shook and slapped him several times. Angel remained limp and unresponsive as Cool Homie shouted, "Angel, wake up. Come on, wake up!" Cool Homie pulled the knitted beanie off his head, pressed his ear against Angel's chest, then delivered a forceful pound with his fist onto Angel's chest. "I said wake the fuck up!"

After he gave Angel a couple of deep mouth-to-mouth breaths and hit his chest again, Trini started dialing on his cell phone. "I'm calling 911. Oh, God, lil' bro, what kinda shit did you end up scoring?"

Homie warned Trini. "And ya better get rid of any fuckin' stash ya got here."

The dispatcher on the line answered, "911, what's your emergency?"

<hr />

The next morning, Minor was seated at a table across from both Julie and Andrea Lifton in a counsel room of Twin Towers Jail. A guard stood in the hallway observing through the surveillance window in the room's wall.

Minor inquired with doubt, "So, Ms. Lifton, you say you want to help Ms. Bulla in my case. Well, how will you be able to clear me?"

Without wasting any time, she explained, "Minor, I'd like nothing more than to see you cleared, but I'm here to make myself available to help your attorney with necessary checks and balances in order to help your case, more or less so that nothing gets overlooked."

Julie reassured him, "Listen, this won't break our lawyer–client privilege. That is to say that our communications will remain confidential and not leave this room. It's so I'm better able to provide candid advice and effective representation. I hope that makes sense to you, Minor."

He leaned back in his chair and shifted his eyes on them. "Yeah, I guess sort of like two heads are better than one."

Andrea smiled as she said, "Mr. Jimenez, I'm glad we're starting to see more eye to eye, and that's a very good way of expressing it."

Julie continued. "Minor, one of our big hurdles deals with your alibi. The prosecution did their homework and came very close to ripping your alibi apart on the stand."

"Yeah, I know that, and I got really upset when you didn't try to do the same to Angel Bernal when he was on the stand."

Andrea interjected, "We all need to be on the same page before you ever get back on the stand to testify, and before we cross-examine Angel Bernal, who's the only eyewitness right now."

"So, is it agreed that Ms. Lifton will assist me in representing you?" Julie asked Minor.

He nodded as he said, "Yes, you both have my consent."

Andrea stood up and extended her hand to him. "Thank you, Minor. We'll stand by you to clear you as innocent." After shaking hands, they both sat back down.

Julie cleared her voice briefly before speaking. "Minor, there is something that your family has confided in me to talk to you about. It's a very personal matter that Anna has asked me to discuss with you."

His mouth gaped open as he said, "Anna asked you to talk to me about something? What is it? Honestly, I've been worried about her lately."

"There's no easy way to tell you this: Anna is pregnant. She's been very hesitant about telling you because of the trial."

"Oh my God, really? Please tell me that she's not going to get an abortion."

"No, she's not. She loves you. Her doctor told her to take it easy for a while, and that's why she won't be coming to your trial for now."

He got up and paced back and forth a few times. Julie stood up and gestured for him to sit back down as the guard in the access area stepped forward and peered through the plate-glass window. "Wow, this is unbelievable. How the hell did this—"

Julie urged him, "Please, sit down. I know this is something both of you must not have planned. Just so you know, her IUD was safely removed, and she's staying at your sister's house for now. She'll be OK."

After he sat down and took a few deep breaths, he said, "Thank God. I think this is all I can take for today, Ms. Bulla."

The guard then opened the door, poked in his head, and asked, "Everything OK here?"

While Julie looked down and saw a message from Dr. Li on her silenced cell phone, she addressed the guard. "Yes, thank you, Officer. And our session was just ending."

He gestured to Minor. "Fine. Let's go, Jimenez."

"Sure, no problem," he told the guard as he rose from his chair. While leaving, he waved to both of his counselors and said, "Bye, Ms. Lifton and Ms. Bulla."

After the guard escorted Minor out of the room, Julie picked up her phone to return the missed call while Andrea said in a matter-of-fact way, "Well, that went as well as can be expected."

"Listen, I'm calling back Dr. Li," Julie told Andrea. "He just left me a message."

After he got on the line, Julie said, "Hello, Dr. Li. This is Julie Bulla. Sorry I missed your call."

"Hello, Ms. Bulla. I think it best to get right to the point. Mario Gutierrez went into cardiac arrest, and we nearly lost him."

"Oh my God, I thought he was stabilizing. When did this happen?"

"Just yesterday. He was improving, but there was an ICU nurse that turned off his alarms before leaving her post for a break. The relief nurse came into his room when he was going into cardiac arrest, most likely brought on by hypoxia."

"Oh, I can't believe it. I hope that nurse was fired."

"Well, she won't be able to work here again, but due to nursing shortages, I don't think her license will be fully revoked. The family is considering changing his code status to No Code if his overall condition doesn't improve."

Julie raised her voice. "You mean *no* more resuscitation?"

"His older sister is acting as head of the family and seeking power of attorney to make that decision."

"Detective Rodriguez notified yet?"

"Yes, he's on his way over to review the situation."

"Thank you, Dr. Li, and I appreciate you keeping us updated."

"No problem. I know this must be a real game changer for everyone. Good luck with this case in court."

In a daze, Julie hung up, then looked at Andrea, who said with a frown, "Sounds like things have taken a bad turn at the hospital."

"Affirmative. Mario's condition has just gone south. I've got to get in touch with Detective Rodriguez by tonight to try to figure out some kind of game plan."

9

Chaos in the Courtroom

It was going on midnight in the emergency room of USC Medical Center. Shortly after the paramedics brought Angel in, he was placed on a respirator under the care of the ER team and thirty-five-year-old Dr. Ravelo. Blood test results of Angel's toxicology screen had just arrived, and an EEG had been ordered as the doctor spoke with Angel's distraught brother, Trini. "Angel's toxicology screening just revealed an extremely high level of a potent narcotic drug in his blood stream. We'll also have to obtain the results of an EEG study in order to determine the level of his brain activity."

"I don't want to see my brother like this, Doctor," Trini said. "Just take him off that breathing machine if he's gonna be a vegetable for the rest of his life."

"Are you his only living relative?"

"Yeah, it's just him and me."

"We're going to transfer him to our medical ICU for now, and someone in charge will speak with you later."

"For God's sake, let him go." Trini curled up in a chair in the corner of the room while hitting his head with his fists.

Once the doctor left the room, an orderly arrived to escort Trini back to the crowded ER waiting room. Cool Homie was seated in the waiting room talking to Driver on his cell phone. "Hey, gotta go. Call you later."

After Trini sat next to Cool Homie, he said, "For fuck sake, Angel ain't ever coming back."

"Dawg, that's fucked up."

Trini stood up in a daze. "I gotta get out of here for a while." Then he asked, "Is Driver around?"

"Yeah, man, he's on his way. Ay, and don't worry. He cleared out your place, so we'll put you up at our place, awright?"

While shaking his head, Trini said, "Where the hell did Angel pick up that shit that took him out?"

After Cool Homie got up and walked with Trini toward the exit, he said, "C'mon! Tell you one thing: pretty sure I know the dude."

"Who?"

"You know who! Termite from Cincinnati Street."

<hr/>

When the trial resumed in the morning, Judge Laura Elliott addressed the members of the court and jury. She looked directly at both counselors behind their tables and asked them, "Are there any pending issues before we proceed with the attempted murder trial of Angel Bernal and Mario Gutierrez versus the alleged-accused, Minor Jimenez?"

Without hesitation, Julie spoke. "Your Honor, may I be allowed to approach the bench?"

With furrowed brows, the judge probed, "Ms. Bulla, do you have any pending issues?"

"Yes, Your Honor. I have critical changes to report to you related to this case."

"Please come forward."

After Julie walked to the bench, Judge Elliott leaned over to listen closely to her. "Your Honor, there's a major change in the condition of Mario Gutierrez that needs to be addressed."

"Are you the only one aware of this change? Is Mr. Fitzgerald aware?"

"Your Honor, I'm fairly sure that the prosecution also has some knowledge of the recent situation."

Judge Elliott called out, "Mr. Fitzgerald, would you please approach the bench?" After he quickly approached, they all huddled together as they began their consultation; meanwhile, everyone in the court waited with bated breath. "All right, counselors, what's this critical issue?"

Fitzgerald spoke first. "Honestly, Your Honor, I was just made aware that Mario Gutierrez had a critical change in his condition through Detective Rodriguez."

Julie said, "Yes, Your Honor. Dr. Li called me with a full medical report of Mr. Gutierrez. He went into cardiac arrest and was resuscitated yesterday. As far as I know, he's still on the ventilator in the ICU."

"Since this issue we're discussing is a new development, I believe today's court proceedings will have to be postponed until the necessary witnesses will be in attendance at our next session. Can we concur on my proposal as the plan of action?"

"Yes, Your Honor," Julie agreed.

Then Fitzgerald pointed out further, "Yes, Your Honor, but may I interject that if Mr. Gutierrez does not survive, the conviction will change to one count of murder in addition to an attempted murder?"

Judge Elliott responded with restraint. "Mr. Fitzgerald, I'm sure you know I am aware, and we will cross that bridge only if we come to it." Then she spoke with composure. "Thank you both. You may return to your tables while I prepare to make an announcement to the court."

Once the counselors returned to their tables, Judge Elliott struck the gavel before making her announcement. "Order in the court. I must address to members of the court that both counselors have brought to my attention a new development related to the victim, Mario Gutierrez, and his condition, which requires further assessment and investigation. We will reconvene this trial and its proceedings after the list of necessary witnesses is made available. Until that date, court is adjourned." She struck the gavel three more times and looked sternly at both Ms. Bulla and Mr. Fitzgerald before rising to leave.

Julie spoke hurriedly with Minor and her associate, Andrea. "I'm not going to lie to you, Minor. The odds have been stacking up against you during these court proceedings, but we do have one last hope."

"I don't see how it can get much worse. Go on, give it to me."

"Mario Gutierrez has been taken out of the medically-induced coma, and Dr. Li informed me that his level of consciousness is improving, but he's still unable to verbalize anything. If he does start to speak again, there's a good chance that he'll identify the real gunman."

"Time's not been on my side. How long can we wait for a miracle?" Minor asked.

"It's a Hail Mary pass, but Detective Rodriguez is ready and waiting for that day at the hospital when Mario's able to cooperate in finding the SOB that shot him down."

To that, Minor said, "I know a high-tech dude from East LA City College who's been working with video transmissions in legal cases when a witness isn't able to be in court. His name is Roberts. We should look him up."

"Yes. Video transmission of court testimony is definitely feasible, especially when the key witness regains consciousness," Andrea said, then she continued. "I can follow-up on that by checking on how soon we can get it arranged."

"Super. We have to get on it now because any change in Mario's level of consciousness will probably improve our chances of the judge approving such a set-up in court," Julie said right before an officer came forward to escort Minor away.

⸺⸻⸺

After the court session, Chris Fitzgerald pounded his fists down on his desk in his office as he raised his voice at his associate, Brian. "I can't believe it. What the hell do you mean that Angel Bernal is nowhere to be found?"

"Just that. I've called his number, and there's no answer. I also checked out the address he lives at with his brother. It's empty," Brian responded.

"We can't lose track of our key eyewitness for this case. For God's sake, get hold of Detective Rodriguez right away. Just who in the hell *is* his brother?"

"His older brother is Trinidad Bernal."

"Well, go and get on it now!" Fitzgerald shouted while his face started to turn red.

Brian began dialing on his cell phone as he got up. After walking out the door, he got an answer on his line. "Hello. I'd like to speak to Detective Rodriguez, please. This is attorney Brian Eckerling from the prosecutor's office, and can you have him call me as soon as he's available? It's urgent."

<hr />

Detective Rodriguez stood in the hall next to the charge RN and looked at Mario in his ICU bed through his room's surveillance window. "So, how's Mr. Gutierrez doing since his cardiac arrest?"

"Well, since Dr. Li ordered to discontinue the IV propofol, he's responding to painful stimuli, and his intracranial pressure and heart rate have been normal," the nurse replied.

"I see you still have him on the respirator. Any chance he'll be breathing on his own?"

"We're in the process of weaning him off the ventilator, but time will tell as we keep checking his arterial blood gases."

"Thank you, Nurse. You've been of great help, and please call me for updates as he improves, OK?"

"Of course, Detective. We have your information. By the way, you mentioned something about placing a police officer outside his door?"

"The department is working on it, but I'll keep your supervisor posted if we get the green light. You have a good day now."

"Thanks. You too."

Detective Rodriguez nodded politely, then walked down the hall toward the double-door exit of the ICU.

Andrea walked into the film and video department equipment room at East LA City College, where twenty-three-year-old Nick Roberts was checking out a video camera to a student with long, dark hair. "There you go, Rocky, and it's due back in two days." The student nodded and left his student ID on the counter before leaving with a Sony PD-150 video camera.

When Andrea stepped up to the counter, Nick greeted her. "Hi. How can I help you?"

"Hi there. You Nick Roberts?" After he gave her a quick nod, she said, "Listen, I'm not a student, but I was referred to you by Minor Jimenez."

He smiled and said, "Oh, yeah, I haven't seen him in a while. How is he?"

"Well, it's kinda a long story. You got a minute?"

"Sure."

"My name is Andrea Lifton, and I'm representing him in a legal case. Basically, we are in need of someone who has experience with video transmissions for court cases when witnesses are unable to be present to testify in court."

"Yes, I've assisted in such cases. How soon do you need my help?"

"It could be as soon as next week. Can our legal team count on you?"

"Of course, count me in, especially if it's going to help out Minor."

Andrea pulled out her card and gave it to Nick, then asked him, "So, when can we discuss the ins and outs with you in detail?"

"My day off is tomorrow. Is that soon enough for you?"

"Yes, thank you, and let's do it tomorrow. How about in the morning at my office?"

Nick nodded in agreement as he looked at her card.

❦

In the LA Police Department, Brian stood next to Detective Rodriguez, hounding the detective as he was going through the file cabinet in his office. "Detective, what the hell's going on with Angel Bernal? He's nowhere to be found. Can't you give us any information on his whereabouts?"

"Really haven't kept tabs on him lately. I know he was staying with his brother. Did you try calling him? You guys should have his address."

"Yeah, no answer. We looked around, and the place has been vacated. Better get an APB out on him."

"We'll check it out. For now, we're keeping close tabs on Gutierrez and his condition. So, you and Fitzgerald will have to hang tight." The detective slammed his file drawer shut and started to head out the door while brushing off Brian. "I'm sure you can see your way out."

<hr />

The criminal courtroom audience was in full attendance as Judge Elliott called the court to order. "Any pending issues before we begin with court proceedings?"

Julie was the first one to speak. "Your Honor, Detective Rodriguez is not here. Mainly, he's been in the ICU room with Mr. Gutierrez, as we speak. Your Honor, due to the current situation, I would like to make a proposal since we are nearing the phase of closing arguments soon."

"What are you proposing, Ms. Bulla?"

"I propose we arrange for video transmission through our technology department in order to present the improving condition of Mario Gutierrez and his possible testimony to members of the court."

Fitzgerald stood up abruptly and said, "Your Honor, I object on the grounds of relevance. At this point in time, Mario's barely conscious, and resorting to video transmission as a means of reliable testimony should not *even* be considered for approval."

"Well, Ms. Bulla, please enlighten us as to how and when such an arrangement can be implemented before I sustain the prosecution's objection."

"Your Honor, video-transmission testimonies in courts have received several approvals nationwide over the last five years in precisely these types of conditions, where the witness is unable to be present to testify during trial proceedings. Currently, Mario happens to be regaining consciousness, and our technology department just needs your approval. It can be initiated, as soon as today, through their assigned outsourced technicians."

"Under these unusual conditions related to this court trial, I will approve your proposal today, Ms. Bulla." Then Judge Elliott faced Fitzgerald and said, "Prosecution's objection is overruled."

"Thank you, Your Honor," Julie said as her tense stance began to lessen.

"We will reconvene this trial as soon as the court is fully equipped for video transmission from the ICU room of Mario Gutierrez. Court is adjourned until further notice of that feasible time frame."

Juror Seven, the older woman, spoke in a lowered voice to another jury member next to her. "Oh my, this is one heck of a trial. Who knows what's going to happen next."

The bailiff instructed the jurors, "Come along, and no talking, please."

―――⚬⚬⚬―――

The following day in the courtroom, Nick Roberts, dressed like a Geek Squad guru from Best Buy, positioned a wide-screen TV showing an image of Mario Gutierrez sitting up in his ICU bed. Mario's eyes were open; his left hand lay on a bible held by a sheriff's deputy who stood off to his side.

After Mario nodded yes to being sworn-in, Julie began to question him. "Mario, do you remember being shot on November seventh?"

On the screen facing the members of the court, Mario clearly nodded without speaking.

Julie said, "Your Honor, please let it be recorded that the witness has nodded his head up and down in response to the question."

"Yes, counselor, it is noted and will be recorded. You may proceed."

"Mario, do you know who shot you?"

He nodded again while struggling to speak with slow pronunciation. "Te-ter-ter-mye-ite …"

"Mario, are you trying to tell us the name of the person that shot you?"

His voice became stronger and screech-like. "Yee-aaah …"

The screen suddenly turned black, and the audio cut out. Nick rushed in and adjusted the settings, to no improvement. Everyone began to speak with each other. Then Fitzgerald stood up with his fists clenched on his desk and yelled, "Your Honor, I object, on the grounds that his testimony can't possibly be submitted."

"Overruled. I call for an hour recess before we reconvene." Judge Elliott struck the gavel three times while voice levels greatly increased in the courtroom.

10

When Lives Collide

After a rather lengthy recess, the court reconvened, and Julie got ready to give everything she could to this case. "Your Honor, I'd like to call Detective Rodriguez back to the witness stand."

As Detective Rodriguez swiftly took the stand, Judge Elliott spoke directly to him. "Detective, I must remind you that you are still under oath."

"Yes, Your Honor."

After he sat in the witness stand, Julie's eyes met Minor's intense stare before she began her questioning. "Detective, were you in the ICU room with Mario Gutierrez moments ago today as he testified under oath?"

"Yes, I was."

"Will you please give us your opinion of his testimony and whether you were able to question him further?"

"In my opinion, Mario Gutierrez is now considered a credible eyewitness. His testimony is crucial to this case. I questioned him further, and when I showed him mugshots, he identified Juan Diaz, aka Termite, a gang member of the Cincinnati Street Kidz, as the gunman."

"Are there other clues or motives that lead you to believe that Juan Diaz attempted to murder Mario and his partner, Angel?"

"Mario pointed to a tattoo with the letters $C K$ on the right side of Diaz's neck in his mugshot, and he wrote the same letters on a drawing of a shirt when asked what the suspect was wearing. These are gang-related signs affiliated with the Cincinnati Street Kidz of Boyle Heights. My instincts tell me the motive stems from gang-rivalry revenge against members of the Forever Boyle Avenue Gang, of which Mario Gutierrez is a member."

"Thank you, Detective. No further questions, and at this point in time, I will make my request to call Angel Bernal back to the witness stand as soon as possible, Your Honor."

Before Detective Rodriguez was asked to step down from the stand, he faced the judge and said, "Excuse me, Your Honor, but we haven't been able to locate Angel Bernal lately, and an all-points bulletin was just sent out for him." Fitzgerald and Brian looked at the judge as though their tails were between their legs, whereas at the defense table, Julie, Minor, and Andrea appeared surprised as hell.

The next day while in his office, Rodriguez received a copy of the APB report with Angel Bernal's whereabouts on his desk. He grabbed his coat and rushed out of his office while dialing Fitzgerald's office on his cell phone.

"Hi. Chris Fitzgerald, please," he asked the female receptionist on the line. After she told him that Fitzgerald wasn't in, he said, "This is Detective Rodriguez. Would you please have him call me as soon as possible? He has my number." Before hanging up, he added, "Or have his associate, Brian, call me. It's urgent."

After arriving at USC Medical Center, Rodriguez went directly to the ICU, where Angel Bernal had been reportedly located as an admitted patient. Rodriguez stood next to Angel's young primary nurse, who was wearing light blue scrubs, in front of a counter lined with several cardiac monitors. She told him the lowdown. "Shortly upon Angel's admission to the ICU, his brother, Trini, who's next of kin, requested that Angel be placed on a No Resuscitation."

After he raised his eyebrows, he replied, "We are going to need to talk to his brother. Do you expect him to be back?"

"I'll have to refer you to our charge nurse if you want more information, Detective. She'll be back in the unit in about an hour."

There was a ring on Rodriguez's cell phone. He silenced it, then excused himself. "Thank you, Nurse. I'll return later to speak to her."

"OK, no problem."

After leaving the ICU, he looked down at his cell phone and returned the missed call from Brian while in the waiting room. "Brian, it's Detective Rodriguez. Thought you should know that we located Angel Bernal."

"No shit, really? Where?"

"He's just down the hall from Mario Gutierrez here at the USC Medical Center ICU. And he's in real bad shape."

"What do you mean?"

"He's been diagnosed as clinically brain-dead due to a drug overdose."

"How the hell did that happen?"

"Don't know, but we need to figure out how to get hold of his brother, Trini, in order to question him. That could take awhile."

"Thanks, Detective. This changes everything. Surely, we'll know more sooner or later."

"No doubt. Keep you posted, as I believe his hospital bed may turn into a stakeout to locate his brother."

"Yeah, he's another person of interest now. Chris isn't going to believe this one."

"Gotta go."

"OK."

In a seedy Westlake District hotel, Termite walked past the lobby, then upstairs to his room on the second floor. After opening the door, he pulled out his .38 Special and placed it next to another pistol on top of a chest of drawers. He then turned and looked out the window facing the street below, and sat on the bed to stroke the ass of his eighteen-year-old girlfriend, Lydia, who was slumbering wearing a black bra and panties from Victoria's Secret. "Hey, mama, you wouldn't believe how much I missed you."

She stretched out while rolling over toward him. "Mmmm, where'd you go?"

"Just out doin' what I do. Ya know how I have ta hustle so we can have our fun together." He laid down a line of coke on a small mirror on top of the end table, then snorted it up with a straw.

While yawning, she said, "Ohhh, let's do it before we go out."

Termite pulled off his jacket and black Calvin Klein T-shirt. After he dropped his jeans, a tattoo with the wording *Love Muscle* and an arrow pointing downward was revealed right above his pubic area. Without hesitation, he mounted himself on top of her. Their loud moans quickly followed as the bed frame began to rock back and forth against the wall.

A man in the next room banged on the wall several times while shouting, "Hey, knock it off over there!" Termite lifted his head, then looked over at the guns on top of the chest of drawers, and as Lydia started to come, she pulled him down closer to her.

<hr />

Thirty-five-year-old undercover officer, Crystal Kendal, dressed in a navy-colored smock, pushed a housekeeping cart past Angel's hospital room. She parked the cart nearby before entering a staff restroom. After closing the door, she got on her cell phone to report to the LAPD. "Officer Kendal here, and there's still no sign of Trini Bernal. No telling if he'll show." She momentarily flushed the toilet and turned on the faucet before ending the call. "Yes, sir, I'll alert you the minute he appears. Out for now."

The on-duty officer who took the call from Officer Kendal entered the office of Detective Rodriguez and said, "Detective, thought you should know the latest reported by the officer on the stakeout at the ICU of USC."

"Yes. How's it going since this morning? Any luck?"

"Sorry, sir. No sign of Trini Bernal, not yet."

"All right, we'll give it another day or so in hopes that he'll show. Thank you."

"No problem. Good night."

———

The next day, Detective Rodriguez and a forty-year-old officer were in a patrol car en route to USC Medical Center. The officer turned off the siren after he parked next to the ER entry. Before getting out of the car, he connected with Officer Kendal. "OK, we're coming up through the ER right now. Just keep Trini Bernal detained until we get up there."

Detective Rodriguez and the officer rushed through the ER and were given no flack by the working hospital staff after Rodriguez flashed his badge. "Let's go," Rodriguez told the officer after the elevator door opened.

Upstairs in a secluded room of the ICU, Officer Kendal stood over Trini, who was slumped in a chair. Rodriguez rushed in with his badge still in his hand while the LAPD officer stood near the partially opened door. "Trini Bernal, I'm Detective Rodriguez from the LAPD. How you doing?"

"C'mon, Detective, does it have to be like this? Ya gonna interrogate me just for seeing my brother before they pull the plug?"

"Nah, nah, Trini; it's nothing like that. Believe me, we just want to get to the bottom of why your only brother ended up like this. Someone's behind it, and I think you know who."

A steady stream of tears ran down Trini's face. "What's it to you? He's my brother, so why should you care? You think I wanna put my life on the line for you just so you can get a promotion for solving this case?"

"Listen, nobody's going to twist your arm here, but you must know that the head gang members behind this will be coming after you next. As Angel's brother, you need our protection because most likely, you're on their hit list."

"Shit, you don't think I know that? So what the fuck's your plan?"

"Help us find these bastards, and we'll set you up with the U.S. Marshals in their Witness Protection Program. They've had a 100 percent success rate of protecting nine thousand witnesses and ten thousand of their family members for over fifty years."

"Let me go back in to say goodbye to my baby brother first. Then we can talk, awright?" Trini wiped away his tears, then glared up at Rodriguez. "I just signed off for the doctors to take him off that breathing machine. There's nothing more they can do to bring him back."

"Officer Kendal, please take him over to his brother," Detective Rodriguez instructed. "I'll go out to talk to Angel's nurse."

"Yes, Detective," Kendal said. Then she told Trini, "Come on, Trini. Let me take you to your brother now." While she escorted him to Angel's room, Detective Rodriguez spoke quietly to the LAPD officer near the doorway and instructed him to closely watch over Trini and Angel.

Once Trini was next to his brother, he knelt over Angel in his bed. Angel's young nurse stood next to Trini, touched his back, and said, "Trini, we are going to turn off the respirator, so Angel will only be receiving a low amount of oxygen right now." The detective and respiratory therapist were also in the room. After all the alarms on the respirator and monitors were turned off, the respiratory therapist turned off the respirator. Then he disconnected Angel's breathing tube.

Trini's gaze fully remained on Angel as he spoke. "I know, I know! Hey, Angel, I'm here. It's Trini. I'm not leaving you, baby brother."

The cardiac wavelength on the monitor changed in rhythm and rate over a few minutes. After Angel went into asystole, the nurse checked his pulse. Then she bent down to hold Trini's hand before saying, "He's gone. I'm so sorry, Trini."

He began to bawl uncontrollably while still positioned over Angel's body, then he shouted, "God, no! No, you're gone. I can't believe you're gone." Detective Rodriguez bowed his head while the two officers watched from the hallway through the room's surveillance window.

Twenty-four hours later, Detective Rodriguez found himself in a heated confrontation with Fitzgerald in his prosecution office. As they stood face-to-face, their voices became louder. "Come on, Rodriguez. You want me to call on the U.S. Marshals to have Angel Bernal's brother receive protection just so he can discredit my only credible witness's sworn testimony. You out of your mind?"

"Listen, Fitzgerald, I know you want to win another case so you can move up the ladder. Just be aware that sometimes what appears to be the truth on the front end doesn't always pan out that way in the end."

"What the hell does that mean? Get real. This theory of yours about Angel being manipulated by rival gang members is way up in the air. Now that Angel's dead from an overdose—and believe me, it looks pretty accidental—you want me to throw out his signed sworn affidavit and court testimony?" He shook his head at Rodriguez, then loosened his tie as he insisted, "Not gonna happen, not on my watch. You got that?"

"All right, all right, but we will continue with our investigation because this case is beginning to open up more and more as we speak."

"And Mario Gutierrez can't be trusted. Not only can anyone decipher his speech, he's got a record longer than the LA River."

"While we're working on leads to locate Diaz as another probable suspect, I'm working on getting Trini Bernal to agree to a polygraph." Rodriguez started to cool off as he bowed his way out of the office.

Then Fitzgerald started to place a call on his desk phone to his associate while yelling out, "You better inform me if and when that's on the schedule, Detective."

"Sure thing, no problem. Bye."

After he got an answer on the phone, Fitzgerald said, "Hi, Brian. I need you to do some groundwork with the U.S. Marshals. Rodriguez is in the middle of screwing up things. He's requesting to place Bernal's brother in the Witness Protection Program as an informant." Before slamming down the phone, he shouted, "Yeah, that's right! So, get on it *now*!"

11

Finding Leads

Seated behind his desk, Detective Rodriguez confronted Trini, who was slouched in a chair on the other side of the desk. The sun was shining brightly through the Venetian blinds of his office window. "OK, Trini, this is how it works: in order for us to give you protection through the U.S. Marshals, we gotta have you agree to a polygraph. But I want you to know that I believe you've been honest with me."

"Yeah, man, this will never end till these fuck-faces get put away. Can you promise me you'll do that?"

"If we arrest Diaz, I will work closely to have him prosecuted to the fullest extent of the law, but for starters, we need some leads on where we can find Diaz. Do you know where he hangs out?"

"I can tell you this: he's a nomad, and nobody really knows where he is on any given day. But I do know that he checks into lots of hotels."

"How about we begin with a list of some hotels? Which district is his favorite?"

"Uh, try the Westlake District first. I know he does a lot of drug runs from there."

Outside, gray clouds were moving in and shut out the sunlight in the room as it started to rain. Rodriguez walked to the window to look overhead, then said, "Guess the storm's coming just as they reported earlier today."

———✦✦✦———

Later that day, Detective Rodriguez paid a visit to Judge Laura Elliott, who was seated behind a huge oak desk in her court chambers. After he handed her a form, she looked it over as he said, "Judge Elliott, this is the signed sworn affidavit by Trinidad Bernal."

"All right, Detective. I suppose you'll be requesting a warrant in the near future."

"Well, yes, we're planning a stakeout close to an area the suspect has been reported as frequenting."

"Good luck, Detective Rodriguez. I'll await your call in the meanwhile."

"Thank you, Judge Elliott."

———✦✦✦———

It was another day of pounding the cement for Rodriguez, as he was following up on possible leads from Trini to locate Termite. In plain clothes, he entered a seedy hotel in the Westlake District, where he approached the middle-aged clerk with glasses who was behind the lobby counter, reading a paperback book. "Excuse me, is the manager available?"

"He's in his office, down the hall," the clerk said while pointing to the left.

"Thanks."

Upon arriving at the closed door labeled *Manager*, Rodriguez knocked a couple of times. A stocky man in his fifties opened the door. "Excuse me, are you the manager?" Rodriguez asked him.

"Yes. Who are you?"

"I'm Detective Rodriguez, LAPD. I have a few questions I hope you can answer."

The man stroked his thin hair with his fingers, then allowed Rodriguez into his office after he showed him his badge. "Oh yeah, is this about the gunshots heard here the other night? Listen, we're keeping an eye out in case that customer shows up again."

Rodriguez raised his eyebrows while he asked, "Can you describe the individual, or do you have his name?"

"You must know, Detective, that in this part of town, there are many who don't use their real names."

"Where were the shots heard? Any visible bullet holes in the hotel?"

"It was in one of the rooms on the second floor. I'll take you up there now if you like."

"Sure, let's go. But first, can anybody give a description?"

"The night clerk said the guy who stayed in that room was a bald Latino with a bunch of tattoos, kinda the usual around here."

Rodriguez's eyes widened as the manager led him out of the office and into the hall. When they arrived in the hotel room on the second floor, the manager pointed to a bullet hole in the wall above the bed. Then Rodriguez looked at it long and hard. "Can you open up the next room?"

The manager pulled the keys from his front pocket and walked toward the door. "Sure. Follow me."

Rodriguez followed him to the next room. After the manager unlocked the door, he opened it for Rodriguez, who stepped in and went directly to the bullet hole in the wall. Then he looked downward to follow an invisible trail that led to a bullet lying below on the carpet. He stared at it, bent down to look closer, and then stood up.

"Did you find something, Detective?"

"Yes. I'm going to have to ask you to close off these two rooms for a while, OK?"

"Sure, I guess so."

"Thanks. And please, keep quiet about this for now. We don't want to create any disturbances with your business as usual. I'll be calling another officer to help gather up some of this evidence soon."

"Whatever you say, Detective."

⸻⸻

In the late afternoon, at the law office of Lifton and Associates, Julie and Andrea were seated on a leather couch, drinking chardonnay. "Listen, Julie, I know you asked me to give you some of my expert assistance in this case, but I must tell you what you really need is an overall makeover in order to win back your client's freedom."

Julie was starting to feel a buzz as she replied, "Oh yeah? Then go ahead and enlighten me with your plan. Pray tell."

"This is no joke. You've got to stop getting behind the eight ball and put more spin in your serve when you get up to present your evidence in court."

"What evidence?"

"That's what I mean! You better get the hell out there and shake it up to gather whatever evidence you can, then fiercely present it before that hard-ass prosecutor does."

"All I got is Mario Gutierrez waking up out of coma land and—"

Andrea interrupted her. "And yeah, do you really think anybody is going to consider him a credible witness? He can barely speak and probably can't even read or write." Then she asserted further, "Please, move on! You should be sticking like glue to Detective Rodriguez. I'm sure he's out there right now looking for other leads or suspects. How about Angel, now that he's MIA? I'm sure that's not sitting well with the prosecution."

Julie acted as though a light bulb had just gone on in her head as she said, "Goddamn it, I know you're right. I've gotta get Rodriguez to give me more of the inside info of what's really going on out there."

Andrea filled up their glasses, then said, "Also, we are going to have to get you into a more dress-for-success wardrobe. Oh, and don't forget, you still need to get laid."

While Julie awkwardly finished a sip, she couldn't help but agree with Andrea's suggestion. "I know, I know." As Andrea left the room, Julie watched the sun setting through the window. Then she began to fantasize about making hot love with a mysterious man on top of the defense table of a darkened courtroom.

～◦/◦/◦～

Feeling motivated after her talk with Andrea, Julie strolled into the office of Detective Rodriguez the following day. He was behind his desk and up to his elbows in shit to do.

"Hi, Ms. Bulla. What can I do for you? Sorry, but I'm swamped and was just getting ready to leave now. Can't really talk. You understand, right?"

She noticed that he had a scar on his left cheek just below his eye and got a little turned on before she said, "Hi, Detective. I won't keep you, but, well, I heard you've been really hard at work with our case. You must be building up a ton of leads by now." Then she asked, "Can you please share with me any information about Angel Bernal? Has he been located yet?"

"As a matter of fact, Angel Bernal was admitted into USC's Medical Center with an overdose of opioids, and his brother consented to have him taken off life support. It's tragic; there was nothing they could do. He was brain-dead."

"Oh my God, do you think it was a suicide or an accidental overdose?"

"It could have been any number of things. Right now, I'm questioning his brother, who happens to be cooperating. Hopefully, we can get to the bottom of it soon."

"Please contact me about anything of significance. I realize that you must work closely with the prosecution.

Listen, I'm sure you have your instincts, and you must know I have mine."

"OK, Ms. Bulla. By the way, you're probably aware that Mario was just placed in a step-down critical care unit. Maybe his mental status will continue to improve over time."

"That's what I heard, and I know it will take more rehab before his speech returns intact. Thank you, Detective. I don't want to keep you, and good luck."

Looking at his watch, Rodriguez headed out the door, and Julie followed behind as he politely told her, "Thanks. Well, I must get going now."

<hr />

Shortly afterward, Detective Rodriguez walked into a polygraph testing room of the LA Police Department. Trini was hooked up to a polygraph while the technician seated next to him began to initiate the test. The technician gave Rodriguez a nod as a signal to start the questioning.

"Are you Trini Bernal?"

"Yes."

"Who is your only brother?"

"Angel Bernal."

"Were you told by your brother, Angel Bernal, that Termite shot him and Mario Gutierrez on November seventh?"

"Yes."

"Did your brother tell you that he lied in court about Minor Jimenez shooting him and Mario?"

"Yes."

"Can you state the reason why Angel had lied and didn't admit who really shot him?"

At this point, there were no extreme fluctuations on the polygraph recording before Trini replied, "Because he didn't want Termite coming back to kill him?"

Meanwhile, Fitzgerald and Brian stood behind the two-way mirror in the adjacent surveillance room. After the technician turned off the polygraph, Fitzgerald continued staring at Trini, then told Brian, "Well, I guess we'll get the results in due time."

"Yeah, I suppose Rodriguez really bit his teeth into this one," Brian said.

"What do you mean?"

"He's been working on some leads to bring in this so-called Termite."

Fitzgerald stamped his foot down, then yelled, "For Christ's sake! What the hell is he up to *now*?"

Outside of another run-down hotel in the Westlake District, Termite, wearing a Chargers jersey, just walked down the street, opened the hotel door, then headed inside to the lobby. Parked across the street, Detective Rodriguez and a thirty-five-year-old undercover officer were seated in a four-door sedan with tinted windows.

"That's him—Juan Diaz," Rodriguez told his partner. Before getting out of the car, he instructed the officer to go over after connecting with backup. Rodriguez walked across the street to the hotel entry, then tailed Termite up to the second floor.

After Termite entered room 28, Rodriguez waited until his partner and backup police arrived upstairs. He banged on the door after the three armed officers filed into the hallway. Then he loudly announced, "Police! Open the door."

When there was no response, Rodriguez turned the knob, then kicked open the door. Termite fired a shot through the doorway as Rodriguez stood away from the door, then shouted, "Give it up, Diaz! We've got a warrant for your arrest. Don't be stupid. Throw out your weapon; then put your hands up, and nobody has to get hurt."

A gun came flying out past the doorway. An officer in bulletproof protection, with his handgun pointed forward, cautiously scoped through the door. The armed officer covered Termite, who had his hands fully raised. Termite was forced face-down to the floor, then cuffed and frisked by another officer.

"Juan Diaz, you're under arrest for the attempted murder of Mario Gutierrez and Angel Bernal. You have the right to remain silent," Rodriguez continued reciting the Miranda rights. Then the officer frisking Termite pulled out a large clear bag of white pills and a packet of white powder tucked under Termite's clothes. He threw both over to another officer and said, "Get that shit secured for evidence."

12

The Verdict

Early morning in the criminal courtroom, Judge Elliott was making her opening announcement to the court and jury members while Chris Fitzgerald and his associate, along with Julie Bulla, Minor, and Andrea, were seated at their tables. "The time has arrived in which both legal counselors will present their closing statements to all of you."

Minor's mother, sister, and boss, Raymundo, were seated in the first row, staring intensely at the judge as she spoke. "Members of the jury, you have been presented all of the existing evidence related to this case. You also heard the testimonies from the witnesses that both the defense and the prosecution brought forward for examination and cross-examination. We will now listen to the closing statements from the prosecution and the defense attorneys of this trial in which the defendant, Minor Jimenez, has been accused of attempted murder of Mario Gutierrez and Angel Bernal."

Judge Elliott then turned her head to face Fitzgerald. "We will begin with the prosecution. Mr. Fitzgerald, would you please proceed with your closing statement?"

He stood up and replied, "Yes, thank you, Your Honor." He walked up to the jury box to address each member. "Ladies and gentlemen of the jury, you have been presented with a simple criminal scenario during this trial; both Mario Gutierrez and Angel Bernal were shot by a gunman. The defendant, Minor Jimenez, was identified as shooting both of the victims in Hollenbeck Park on November seventh. Now, the time has come to review the facts that have been presented to you throughout this trial."

He raised one of his arms briefly as he continued. "Forget about what you've seen on TV and in the movies. Fact—Angel Bernal, one of the victims, gave a sworn eyewitness testimony on the stand that the defendant shot him, then fled the scene. Fact—Detective Rodriguez arrested Minor Jimenez and placed him in a lineup where Angel Bernal again confirmed that Minor Jimenez was the gunman. Fact—Minor Jimenez was in a public restaurant where he openly threatened both of the victims' lives during a fight just days prior to the shooting. And Mr. Jimenez was unable to confirm his true whereabouts on the actual day and time of the shooting during his testimony on the stand."

Fitzgerald slowly walked past each jury member, then glared at Minor, who was holding a Saint Christopher medal under the table. "And what has the defense provided as facts? Well, they brought forward last-minute witnesses to confuse you in an attempt to distract you from arriving at a fair, decisive verdict. The condition of Mario Gutierrez continues to hang by a thread at USC Medical Center. His testimony by a poorly transmitted video should have been thrown out of court. You saw how he could barely communicate. He's not a credible witness, and who knows if he'll ever be able to testify due to the sustained injury to his brain. Bringing forth Trini Bernal as a witness recently to discredit the testimony of his recently deceased brother, Angel, is nothing but a cheap trick to get the defendant off the hook." He lifted up one of his fists while raising his voice. "Both Mario Gutierrez and Trini Bernal have long criminal records, whereas Angel Bernal had no history of breaking the law. I implore each of you to take a close look at the credibility of the witnesses, and to search your conscience about whose testimony you should honestly trust as you collectively determine your verdict."

Once again, Fitzgerald glared at Minor as he walked to his table. "Thank you, members of the jury, for your dedication, and thank you, Your Honor," he said while he stood behind his table.

"Thank you, Mr. Fitzgerald," the judge said before addressing Julie. "Ms. Bulla, would you please proceed with your closing statement for the defense?"

Julie, who was dressed in a blue Versace dress suit, stood up, then walked forward to the jury box as she responded, "Yes, and thank you, Your Honor. Ladies and gentlemen of the jury, there is no doubt that all of you have demonstrated a great deal of dedication through your valued service during this highly volatile attempted-murder trial. And now, it's time to get down to the brass tacks, or rather, the meat and potatoes of this entire trial. You just heard the prosecution rehashing the initial phase of the trial, which concentrated on one victim's sworn testimony and an insufficient alibi provided by my defendant, Minor Jimenez. All the while, the other victim, Mario Gutierrez, remained unresponsive an ICU bed. Please bear with me as I recap with each of you the tremendous amount of evidence presented in this court through the in-depth investigation of the LAPD, which was led by Detective Rodriguez, over the duration of this trial."

Julie gained the heightened attention of the jurors, the prosecution, and her client. She began to get on a roll as Detective Rodriguez, in the back row, looked at her, then at his watch. "All of you viewed the video-transmitted testimony of Mario Gutierrez from his hospital bed after he regained consciousness; that was not staged, and he was not coaxed. And Detective Rodriguez testified that he questioned him further to determine a possible suspect other than the alleged-accused, Minor Jimenez. Next, the other suspect, Juan Diaz, was determined through his mugshot and the gang-related tattoo, as pointed out by Mr. Gutierrez. Secondly, Angel Bernal, the initial sole eyewitness, is now deceased due to a drug overdose. Now, through a polygraph test, it was confirmed that his only brother, Trinidad Bernal, stated that Angel had confessed to him that Minor Jimenez was not the gunman. Why did his younger brother, Angel, lie in court? Because he feared for his life, and because if he ever told the truth, the rival gang members would make sure he'd never squeal or utter another word again. Please put your minds at rest because Juan Diaz is now in custody, thanks to the LAPD and Detective Rodriguez, who has remained in charge of this case. Also, during the arrest of Diaz, two .38 Special handguns were in his possession, and the bullets fired by him at the scene of the arrest were recovered as evidence. Both of the victims just so happened to have been shot with bullets from a .38 Special pistol."

At a slow pace, she looked into the eyes of each juror as she continued. "Whether Angel's death was a suicide, an accidental overdose, or an actual homicide is questionable at this point because that investigation remains ongoing. Just let me leave you with this—the narcotic drug fentanyl, which showed up in Angel's toxicology report before his death, was also the drug seized in a sizable quantity that was in the possession of the suspect, Juan Diaz, during his recent arrest."

Julie stepped away, then stood behind Minor before she closed. "Ladies and gentlemen of the jury, as you weigh all of the evidence brought forward and decide your verdict, I strongly urge that you not conclude this trial without first and foremost taking into consideration that Minor Jimenez was wrongly accused. It would be a travesty to convict an innocent man for such a serious crime that he did not commit. Thank you, members of the jury, and thank you, Your Honor."

"Thank you, Ms. Bulla. Members of the jury, you have heard the closing arguments from the prosecution and the defense. At this time, the jury will be allowed to deliberate over the next two weeks. This court trial will reconvene when the verdict has been reached, and the pending trial session will be scheduled for the jury's final announcement." She struck the gavel three times before rising from her seat. "Court is adjourned."

<hr />

One week later, in the jury deliberation room of the LA Superior Court building, the head juror, a clean-cut forty-year-old veteran Marine, was seated at a table surrounded by the other jurors as he spoke. "Well, I believe that we can't announce a verdict until the vote is unanimous."

Everyone looked over to the twenty-nine-year-old petite juror, an elementary school teacher in a conservative A-line dress. Then she said, "I really don't know whether he did it or not, but something tells me that he's guilty."

Juror Seven, the older woman seated beside her, probed her for an answer. "Why? Is it because you were convinced by the prosecutor that he did it from the start?"

"Well, yes, maybe so."

"Listen, I know all of you thought I screwed up when I did something stupid and spoke to a witness a while back. Oh, gosh, I felt so ashamed. Well, I just believe in my heart and my head that Detective Rodriguez really knows his stuff. My God, with all the evidence that he recovered, I can't help but be convinced that Minor Jimenez is innocent."

"All right, everybody, I think we'll need to put this to another vote before we come up with a verdict," said the head juror.

⁂

The next day, all the jurors had been seated in the jury box, and Judge Elliott called the court to order, then asked, "Members of the jury, have you reached a verdict?"

The head juror rose from his seat and announced, "Yes, we have, Your Honor."

Judge Elliott asked Minor, "Will the defendant please rise?" After he stood up and faced the jury, she asked the head juror, "What is your verdict?"

He replied, "We, the jury, have found the defendant, Minor Jimenez, not guilty in the crimes of attempted murder of both Angel Bernal and Mario Gutierrez."

The entire courtroom went into an uproar. Julie and Minor embraced; then Andrea rushed forward and patted both of them on the back. Minor's family members hugged him and started to hug each other.

In a moment of panic, Minor asked his sister, Christina, "Where's Anna? Is she OK?"

Filled with tears, she said, "Oh, Minor! Yes, Anna's fine. She wants you to know that she loves you and that she just can't wait to have your baby."

In the back of the courtroom, Detective Rodriguez gave Julie a thumbs-up when she turned in his direction. As Minor looked back at the detective, he noticed his dad standing off to the side in the back row; he hurried back and said to him, "Dad, you're here. You came."

"Yes, Minor, I'm here. How could I not be here for the bravest son any father on earth could ever have?"

"Dear God, how I missed you, Dad."

"Oh, Minor, I missed you too. Please, forgive me." Minor and his father exchanged a sturdy handshake, then gave each other an enormous, long-overdue embrace.

Minor's mother and Christina rushed over to them. Then his mother cried and kissed Minor. After Minor hugged her, he told everyone, "I can't believe I'm really free. Thank God you're all here now. You'll never know how much your belief in me kept me hanging on with every passing day."

Raymundo and Julie came forward to give Minor more hugs and pats on his back as Julie said, "We never stopped believing in you, Minor."

"I know you had my back, Ms. Bulla," Minor replied. "Thank you, with all my heart."

Raymundo stepped in between them and said, "OK, enough now! Minor, your chariot awaits. I'm here to escort you in my Silverado and deliver you to Anna, your lady-in-waiting, who anticipates your presence at your sister's home as we speak."

Minor wrapped his arm around his boss's shoulder as he said, "All right! Just lead the way, Raymundo. I'm right behind you. Let's go!"

THE END

Epilogue

One Year Later

It was a beautiful late morning at St. Mary's Catholic Church. Father Guillermo stood in the baptismal chapel area surrounded by the friends and family members of the Jimenezes during the baptism of Minor and Anna's infant daughter. The godmother, Christina, and the godfather, Raymundo, stood by as Father G poured holy water over their godchild's head. There wasn't any crying coming from the infant, held by her mother, Anna, but there were plenty of tears in the eyes of close family members, including Minor's mother and father.

Father G acclaimed, "With the powers vested in me by the Holy Catholic Church, I bless this child in the name of the Father, the Son, and the Holy Spirit. Amen." Everyone smiled as those in attendance performed the sign of the cross. Then Father G made an announcement. "Goodwill to all and peace be with you. Please join me in the church rectory for fellowship and light refreshments on this glorious day of the baptism of the daughter of Minor and Anna."

Upon arrival to the reception hall, Minor had his arm wrapped around his wife, Anna, who was carrying their baby, dressed in a long white christening gown. Within a few minutes, Christina took her godchild in her arms and carried her over to the grandparents, Mr. and Mrs. Ernesto Jimenez.

During the reception, Julie Bulla and Detective George Rodriguez walked over to Minor and Anna. Then Julie presented a wrapped gift to them. "I'm so happy for both of you, and I hope that your family will be blessed with many years of happiness."

Minor replied, "Ms. Bulla, thank you. You were such a godsend to us during a very dark time in our lives. You will always be in our hearts."

Christina walked over carrying her godchild and said, "Hi, Ms. Bulla. Here she is, Julie Anna Jimenez. Isn't she beautiful?"

Speechless, Julie bowed her head and gently touched Julie Anna's hand. Minor said, "We hope that someday our child will be as conscientious toward justice as the woman that helped free me, her father."

George stepped in closer to Julie and squeezed her shoulder as she began to cry. Then he told the proud parents, "Congratulations. Your child is beautiful, and you must feel like the luckiest parents on earth at this moment."

"Oh, yes, thank you," they both replied without hesitation.

It wasn't long before the others gathered around little Julie Anna, the star of the moment. Raymundo raised his arms as he called out loudly to the group, "I'd like to make an announcement while we are here celebrating little Julie

Anna's baptism, if I could. As you know, my business is a little more than I can handle lately, thanks to all the great work that my employees provide to our growing number of customers. So, I am now promoting Minor to manager of my auto body repair shop, effective as of next week."

After several hoots and pats on Minor's back from several friends and family members, Julie and George clapped alongside everyone. Then they headed outside together. George began to reflect on his last year with her as they started down the walkway. "Well, Julie, I believe you have touched the lives of many of these people in a very special way."

"Listen, George, you must know that I wouldn't have been able to represent Minor as effectively to prove he was not guilty without the amazing detective work you headed."

"Don't discount yourself, Counselor. It was you and your dedication to prove Minor's innocence that motivated us to give it our all in his defense."

"Well, I know you can't tell all, but did everything work out OK with Angel's brother, Trini, and Mario Gutierrez through the Witness Protection Program?"

"I can tell you this: they are in a place where the East LA gang members will no longer endanger them. Both Trini and Mario have started new lives under different identities; and believe me, they made the right choice to cooperate with us in arresting and convicting the real gunman."

Julie took a deep breath, then leaned on him as she placed her arm under his arm. With a sly grin, she changed the subject. "Hey, George! How about you and I find someplace to have a drink?"

"Sure. I hear there's a local Mexican cafe nearby on Evergreen that serves up a killer margarita."

Before walking any farther, she kissed him on his left cheek, just below his scar, then smiled as she said, "Sounds very inviting. Lead the way. Let's go!"

Author's Note

I began to develop this story in a twenty-paged screenplay for a film-short, then as a full-length feature film. I'd like to acknowledge screenwriting professor, Eric Martinez, for his encouragement during my initial phase of writing. One year later, I completed the Novella version.

My idea and inspiration for the book stems from childhood memories of my mother, who became a single parent after my father died when I was seven-years-old. My three brothers, my sister, and I were raised in a housing development in the Harbor area of Los Angeles. I witnessed the struggles that my family and other families endured when faced with unexpected adversities. Years ago, I remember an incident when one of my older brothers, who was eighteen-years-old at the time, had been accused of a serious offense by a group of three individuals. Several weeks later, the detective investigating the case was forced to withdraw the charges against my brother after the members of the group recanted their accusations.

I truly must give great thanks to my life partner and fiction writer, Robert Torres Gonzales, who was raised in East Los Angeles during his teens then attended *California State University Los Angeles and UCLA*. Sharing his life experiences along with his literary expertise will always remain valuable to me for many years to come.

Most of the events recorded in this book loosely occurred; one or two were experiences of my own, the rest of those of people who I encountered while growing up in the Los Angeles Wilmington Harbor area. Minor Jimenez was drawn from life; and Julie Bulla was also—they were created through a combination of the characteristics of a few people whom I knew and had gone through similar legal experiences.

Some of the gang-related practices touched upon were in use among its members in the surrounding area of East LA during the last few decades, and the names of the gangs and the characters used in this book are fictitious.

Although my book is intended mainly for the enjoyment of crime suspense readers, I hope it will not be disregarded by others on that account, for part of my goal has been to try to remind conscientious individuals of how they may have reacted if placed in the same situational environment. In conclusion, I hope to instill a message with positive impact upon the readers of this book by pointing out that when faced with extreme adversity, may each of your journeys of struggle ultimately bring about courage, love, and kindness instead of fear.

PAULA MCCOLM

LOS ANGELES, 2021

Connect with the author on these Social Media Links:
https://paulamccolm.com
https://twitter.com/mccolmpaula
https://www.facebook.com/paula.mccolm.77

Printed in the United States
by Baker & Taylor Publisher Services